"Other women might fawn all over you...."

"But I'm not one of them Matt Carstairs," Alandra told him hotly.

"And you're not looking for a romantic alliance either, are you?" he scorned.

And then suddenly, while she was still spitting fire, he moved that one step forward and took hold of her.

"We'll prove that, shall we?"

And before his intention had time to register, Alandra felt Matt's mouth come down over hers, and she was then being soundly kissed by the one man she hated before all others.

But suddenly the fire of temper was going out of her, and a fire of a sort she was slow to recognize began to kindle inside her.

"Stop it," she protested, but she had stopped struggling....

Books by Jessica Steele

HARLEQUIN PRESENTS

HARLEQUIN ROMANCES

These books may be available at your local bookseller.

For a free catalog listing all titles currently available, send your name and address to:

Harlequin Reader Service
P.O. Box 52040, Phoenix, AZ   85072-9988
Canadian address: Stratford, Ontario   N5A 6W2

JESSICA STEELE

reluctant relative

Harlequin Books

TORONTO • NEW YORK • LONDON
AMSTERDAM • PARIS • SYDNEY • HAMBURG
STOCKHOLM • ATHENS • TOKYO • MILAN

Harlequin Presents first edition January 1984
ISBN 0-373-10661-0

Original hardcover edition published in 1983
by Mills & Boon Limited

CHAPTER ONE

It was when Alandra Todd alighted at the not-much-more-than-a village station, and approached the porter-cum-station-master, that her plans for the weekend first started to go awry.

'Can you direct me to the nearest hotel?' she enquired of the podgy little man bent over a couple of crates which, besides herself, had been the only objects to leave the train at Ferny Druffield.

'Hotel!' His surprise as he straightened gave her a fair impression that he thought she had horns growing out of her head.

'There *is* a hotel in Ferny Druffield?' she pressed hopefully, but had guessed that there wasn't even before he started shaking his head. 'An inn—a—pub, where I can stay overnight?' she suggested, still hopeful.

'There's only the Crossed Keys and the Social Club,' he responded, eyeing the slender girl, a warm September breeze gently teasing her pale gold hair. 'And they don't take boarders,' he added, not very helpfully.

He went back to inspecting his crates, and Alandra, without being conscious of it, moved her weekend case from one hand to the other as she stood and wondered what to do now.

Had it not been for the last words her mother had spoken to her before she had died a month ago—and *that* letter—she would still be in London. But, having made up her mind to come to Ferny Druffield she had thought to spend the rest of today and some of tomorrow—before she went to Roseacres—in looking around the place where both her parents had once lived.

That she should have checked on overnight accom-

modation first was all too obvious now. Just as it was
obvious that her plans would have to undergo major
reconstruction.

'Is—is there a taxi I could hire?' she asked the bent
back of the railway official, seeing nothing for it but
that she would have to forgo any idea of taking a look
round.

'Depends,' he answered, which she didn't think was
very forthcoming.

'On what?' she asked, putting down her case since it
did not appear that she was going *anywhere* in a hurry.

'On how far you want to go.'

He had straightened again, and Alandra forced a
smile when she had never felt less like smiling.
'Roseacres,' she told him, and saw him take interest.

'You mean the Carstairs and Todd place?'

So that was how Roseacres was known locally—the
Carstairs and Todd place! 'That's where I mean,' she
agreed.

'It's three mile away,' she was enlightened. 'I could
give Jim Lasky a ring—he might take you up there if he
isn't too busy with his prized tubers.'

'I'd be pleased if you would,' smiled Alandra, and
thought that at last she was getting somewhere, when
he trundled off inside the old brick building.

It was bothersome having to go to Roseacres today,
she pondered, as she waited. Just the thought of facing
the grandfather she had never seen made her angry. She
really needed one night in his vicinity at least in which
to collect herself before she saw him.

Thank goodness she had thought to travel in her
linen dress rather than the jeans in her case which she
had been going to change into the moment she had
secured a room for the night. Her dress was of pale
green, with a semi-flared skirt, and was turned into
elegance by being matched with a white polka-dotted
long green silk scarf. It was the smartest garment she
had in her limited wardrobe.

'You're in luck. Jim's on his way,' said the tubby man, coming back and eyeing her weekend case with some curiosity. 'Come after a job, have you?'

'Nothing like that,' she told him, no inclination in her to give him, and most likely the whole village, fuel for gossip, by telling him she was going to Roseacres to see her grandfather. Thoughts of that man were not pleasing. 'I'll go and wait outside,' she said abruptly.

But outside in the station yard, she was to find that the hatred resurrected by just thinking of that man's name was still there, haunting her. Again she was seeing his name in print, written in his hand at the bottom of the letter she had discovered among her mother's possessions. That letter dated six years ago, acknowledging the news her mother had sent him of the death of his son; Alandra's father.

And again, as she waited for her transport, Alandra was reliving the moment when her mother had turned her tired head and whispered, 'Alandra—go to—Roseacres.' She had been surprised, but had readily agreed—would have agreed then to any request.

'I'll go, darling,' she had gently promised, knowing her mother was too weak for her daughter to question why, as she repeated her request, it should suddenly seem so important to her. Her father had left his home twenty-three years ago, stopping on his way only once, and that had been to pick up his beloved Lucy, the frail village girl who was alone as the elderly aunt she had lived with had died. Neither of them had ever returned, which put the question into Alandra's mind of why, when neither of her parents had felt pulled to return to Ferny Druffield, her mother should want *her* to go.

After her mother's death, Alandra had been so grief-stricken that she had barely remembered the promise she had made. But life had to go on, and a week later had seen Alandra sorting through her mother's belongings and, tears running down her face, she had tried to direct her mind into other channels. She would have to do something about getting a job soon, she thought, as she wiped her eyes and packed clothes away. Hector Nolan, her old boss, had been a real friend to her, but he had a new secretary now.

She had gone to work for Hector in the one-man-band insurance business he ran when she had been sixteen. And it had been the greatest stroke of good fortune, her mother having more bad days than good days since her father had died, that when the tenants of the flat above Hector's offices had left, he had offered the tenancy to her. This had meant that she could often pop upstairs to look in on her mother to check that all was well.

It had worked out well too, until the May of this year, when her mother had been taken to hospital with a heart attack from which she had only partially recovered. Alandra could still recall the shock she had felt when, although putting it gently, the doctor had told her that her mother would not see the year out. She had given Hector her notice then, after calculating that their small savings would just about last.

'But you can't leave,' he had protested. 'You've been with me four years. You know where everything is . . .'

'I want to spend more time with my mother,' she had told him, going as far as she could without breaking down and telling him that there was not much time left.

'As bad as that, baby,' said the sandy-haired, forty-two-and-suddenly-fatherly Hector. And she had been hard put to it not to cry when, striving to be strong, she had told him with a watery smile:

'I'll only be upstairs if you run into trouble while training somebody else.'

But she hadn't cried then, and she did not cry until the day of her mother's funeral. And then it was not until she had assured Hector and his wife Bianca that she would be all right, until she had closed the flat door after them, that she had sat down and she had sobbed and sobbed.

She was still crying when, the last of her mother's clothes packed away, she had come across the letter in an old handbag that had never been thrown away simply because, even though old, it might still have a use.

Letters, Alandra considered, were so very personal. She had been in two minds then whether or not to take it out of its worn envelope and read it. But it was the thought that, since no one ever wrote to them, bar the electricity company and the rates department, and with the address on the letter that of their old address, perhaps there was someone she should write to to inform them that her mother had passed away.

Taking the letter from its expensive envelope, she looked first to see who it was from. And as she read the formal signature 'Alain Todd' so her glance shot up to see that the address was 'Roseacres, Ferny Druffield'. It was then that she recalled her promise to 'Go to Roseacres'. But as she read on, and anger took her, so the tears that had seemed to be her constant companion these last few days, dried.

'Madam,' her grandfather had written bluntly, just as though he didn't know that her mother's name was Lucy, when Alandra knew damn well that he did, 'Courtesy decrees I must acknowledge your advice of my son's death. I would, however, remind you that for me Edward Todd ceased to exist on the day when, with complete disregard for his family's feelings, he walked out of his home.'

Aghast at the tone of the letter, Alandra made herself read on. 'As you well know, my son was disowned by me when he turned his back not only on his family to go off with a penniless invalid,' gasping, she read more, 'when he was not competent even to look after himself, much less an ailing wife, but when he also turned his back on his place, his responsibility, in the business.'

Staggered at the cruelty to her mother the missive contained, Alandra just could not believe the final paragraph, and she was consumed by storming rage when again she re-read, 'I can only assume since my son's demise has preceded your own, that your health must have vastly improved. This leaves me to state that should it be in your mind to write to me again, then be assured it will be to no avail. I have no intention whatsoever of giving you the smallest financial support.'

She already knew the signature 'Alain Todd', but she read it again. And with memory fresh in her mind of her good, gentle, fragile mother who had never asked anyone for anything no matter how financially pressed they were—and they had been hard up many times—so hate entered her heart. She hated that this man, who had sired her happy-go-lucky father, should for one moment accuse her mother, whose natural goodness had had her acquainting the old skinflint of his son's death, of being about to beg him for a handout.

The urge to go and tell her grandfather straight away what she thought of him had to be held in check. Her mother, penniless though she might have been, had been a lady. She would not want her charging to Ferny Druffield to give Alain Todd a piece of her mind.

Three weeks later, though still angry whenever she thought about that letter, she had cooled down and was now favouring a letter of her own. A letter to her grandfather acquainting him of her mother's death with a suitably sarcastic postscript to the effect that she would be obliged if he did not offer her financial support, since she was very particular from whom she accepted money.

But, with her mother's death so close, her promise that she would go to Roseacres repeating and repeating in her brain, not withstanding that she didn't have it in her to write anything sarcastic on the same page in which she referred to her mother's death, Alandra decided that the promise she had made should be honoured.

A car that had seen better days rattled into the station yard, and brought her out from her thoughts. 'You the one who wants to go to the Carstairs and Todd place?' asked the thin-faced man who pushed his head out of the open window.

Since she was the only one standing there, Alandra didn't give him very high marks for intuition. 'Just a minute,' she said, 'I want to enquire what time the next train is to London.'

'Six o'clock,' the driver informed her, looking inquisitively at her weekend case.

Thanking him, and not needing to disturb the porter-cum-station-master, she climbed into the apology for a taxi, her mind going ahead to her destination, the thought coming as the car rattled out of the station yard, of how little she knew of her father's family.

She could not recall any in-depth conversations with her father on his family, but somehow, through remembered snatches of conversation, she had the knowledge that her father was not an only child. If memory served, he had a married sister Eunice who, with her husband and baby, had lived at Roseacres twenty-three years ago—Robert, she rather thought the baby had been called, though of course, he would be a grown man by now.

With both the railwayman and Jim Lasky calling Roseacres the 'Carstairs and Todd' place, Alandra stretched further into the recesses of her mind, and for the rest of the journey she put together snippets from either her mother or her father, a picture forming of how it had all begun.

There were bound to be some gaps, she realised, but from what she thought she knew, Grandfather Todd and Granville Carstairs had been a couple of engineers from wealthy backgrounds who had started the Carstairs and Todd business. And, because it seemed that they spent every waking moment down at the factory, their wives, strong-minded both, had put their heads together and had decided that if they were ever to see their menfolk—Grandmother Todd already having produced her babies, Granville Todd's wife having to wait another ten years for her off-spring—then they would move into a house large enough to accommodate not only the two families, but one large enough to have room for an office. That way their men could pore over drawings to their hearts' content, while the women, if not seeing them, could be happy in the knowledge that at least they were at home.

Her taxi seemed to have been winding uphill for some time when, realising that she knew far more about her family than she had thought, Alandra realised too, that Roseacres must be a fairly sizeable property if it was still peopled by the off-spring of both Carstairs and Todd.

But she felt no pleasure in having blood ties with one half of that firm that was now a world-wide name in engineering. All she wanted, as the taxi ceased climbing and turned into a mile-long drive and stopped in front of a tall square solid-looking residence, was to keep her promise made to her mother as she lay dying; to show her face at Roseacres, and to be out of there to catch the six o'clock train back to London.

'Will you wait?' she asked the driver, who seemed in no hurry, and who appeared more interested in the magnificent lawns and flower beds than he was in his fare.

He nodded absently, and Alandra, her features composed, crossed the gravel driveway and mounted the stairs to the stout outer door. In the shade of the pillared porch, she pulled on the door bell and waited. She would not let the memory of that letter make her angry, she decided. Dignified and aloof, that was the way to be. She owed that to her mother's dignified memory.

The front door was opened, and a woman in a dark dress stood there. 'I've come to see Mr Todd,' said

Alandra, not knowing who the woman was, though seeing no resemblance to her father in the woman's. rather plain features, she thought it unlikely that she was her aunt Eunice. 'Mr Alain Todd,' she qualified, unnecessarily, since with her cousin Robert bearing his own father's surname, there was only one Mr Todd likely to be in residence.

'I'm afraid Mr Todd is out,' the buxom lady informed her, but did not offer anything further.

Alandra hesitated, and had to remind herself, when inclination would have had her returning to the taxi and going back to London, that her promise would only plague her and have her making a second journey if she went away now.

'They're all out,' the woman thought to add, looking ready to close the door and get back to whatever it was she had been doing.

Alandra saw it was time she asserted herself. 'And you are?' she enquired, a haughtiness in her tone she didn't know she possessed, be the lady her aunt Eunice, or whoever.

'I'm the housekeeper, Mrs Pinder,' she introduced herself, a puzzlement in her expression as though Alandra's manner was one she recognised from somewhere.

'What time do you expect Mr Todd to return?' Alandra questioned.

'About fourish, I should say, miss,' was the respectful answer.

Checking her watch, Alandra saw it had only just gone three. She then did a quick mental calculation, and reckoned that she could still catch that six o'clock train even if she had to walk the three miles to the station. For a bonus, it was downhill all the way.

'Wait just a moment, would you, Mrs Pinder,' she said, and quickly she returned to her driver, settling up with him. Although since she couldn't be sure what time her grandfather would arrive, she was unable to

ask him to return to pick her up. He was already
rattling away over the drive when, now carrying her
weekend case, Alandra went back to the waiting
housekeeper.

'I'm a relative of Mr Alain Todd,' she was forced to
own. 'I should like to wait until he returns.'

Mrs Pinder looked a shade torn, she saw, and
guessed then that she never allowed entry to anyone
unless she was sure of their pedigree.

'My name is Todd, too,' Alandra smiled, 'and I
assure you I am not here to make off with the family
treasures.'

Her stated name, as much as the new-found authority
she had discovered in herself, Alandra thought, had
Mrs Pinder giving way. But as she crossed the threshold
into a wide thickly carpeted hall, so any sign of the
smile she had given the housekeeper disappeared. She
was in the home of that bitter man who had disowned
his son, and from the tone of his letter, had also tried to
put down his daughter-in-law, and the whole house
seemed alien to her. Just being there felt alien, and had
her wanting to leave without ever having to see that
man who, although they had never met, she felt she
hated.

She saw that Mrs Pinder, having closed the front
door, was beginning to look as though she wasn't very
sure that she had done the right thing.

'I'll wait in the drawing room, if I may,' she told her
as though to the manor born, nothing in her to show
that she had never been in anyone's drawing room
before, only a memory there of the cosy living room she
had shared with her mother.

Alandra pushed her memories to the background as
the housekeeper showed her into a high-ceilinged,
delicately striped wallpapered room. She had no quarrel
with Mrs Pinder, and it seemed incumbent upon her
then to put that good lady at ease.

'Mr Todd will be pleased I have called, I assure you,'

she told her, not believing anything of the sort. He had not wanted to see her father once he had left and, as she saw it, he would have as little time for his son's daughter—and that suited her fine.

The housekeeper looked to be relieved, she saw. But in turn, she had Alandra feeling awkward when she suggested, 'Would you like some tea, Miss Todd?'

She was thirsty, she had to admit, and a cup of tea would have gone down nicely. But she wanted nothing that her grandfather could provide. Then, oh what the hell, she thought, seeing that Mrs Pinder was hovering and might feel better to have some commission. Principles were one thing, but she hoped she was above being petty-minded.

'That would be lovely,' she thanked her graciously. And only then had time to look around the room when Mrs Pinder departed.

Tasteful furniture, she observed, not bothering to take her ease in either one of the chairs or settees spaced around. Tasteful pictures, she noted, going over to inspect one of half a dozen hung on the walls. She turned from the picture, her eyes going slowly round the room. The contrast between this room, this home, the home where her cousin, if he still lived here, her aunt Eunice and her husband, had been brought up, seemed in deep contrast to her own home.

The furniture in the tiny flat she had shared with her mother had been cheap second-hand when they had bought it, and had been furniture they had taken with them when they had moved into the flat over the office. With her mother so frequently ill even when her father had been alive, they had no sooner got on their feet a little when he had had to have time off work to look after the both of them. And since not many employers were prepared to put up with his many absences, for he always put the two of them first, it had meant he was more often without an employer than with one.

Mrs Pinder, coming in with the tea-tray and setting it

down on a low table, had Alandra leaving her thoughts
temporarily, and going to seat herself down by the table.

'Thank you, Mrs Pinder,' she said politely, not
wanting to detain the woman. 'This will keep me going
until Mr Todd returns.'

Left to herself again, Alandra poured tea into the
shell-like china of a teacup, her mind going to resume
her thoughts. She had been nearing fourteen, Alandra
remembered, when her parents had started to get on
their feet again and she had been able to give a hand in
caring for her mother—the odd day or week off school
never that important—when, with all the odds against
her father dying first, he had caught pleurisy, followed
by complications because he had gone back to work too
soon, and suddenly, the light-hearted, laughing-eyed
man was no longer there. Tears started to prick as she
recalled how utterly distraught her mother had been in
those early days.

Then all at once she heard a door open, and voices in
the hall, combined with other muffled sounds. And hate
was back with her. No place now for tears. Soon, she
knew, another twenty minutes to go before the hour
struck four, she would be face to face with the man who
had disowned her father and had tried to disown her
mother.

Cold anger struck as, that letter her grandfather had
written indelibly printed in her mind, Alandra returned
her cup and saucer to the tray. She sat elegantly in the
wide well-padded chair, her suitcase to the side of her,
one elbow resting negligently on the edge of her chair,
her hands linked in her lap, her legs neatly crossed at
the ankles. To anyone observing her, it would appear
that she was poised, relaxed, and very much at home
with the tea-tray near at hand should she require a
second cup, the china bearing evidence that she had
already partaken from the teapot beneath the cosy.

Alandra thought she heard the higher pitched tones
of the housekeeper, then the rumble of deeper tones.

And as the handle of the door her eyes were fixed on slowly began to turn, so her chin tilted that fraction higher so that should anyone think that she was in any way a lesser mortal than any of her father's family, then they would very soon learn differently.

But the man who pushed open the drawing room door, and with an arrogance that said he didn't care who heard him in conversation, left it open, was not the nearly seventy-year-old man she had calculated her grandfather must be.

Nor, as for a long moment the tall athletically-built dark-haired man stared at the cool look of her, was he her cousin, she thought. Robert, if she had worked it out correctly, should be twenty-three or four now—this man, who without yet having said a word, and who gave her the impression that he was taking her apart piece by piece, looked to be in his middle thirties, which ruled him out as her cousin's father, too.

Still without speaking, the dark-haired man came further into the room, Alandra's green eyes following him as she saw his glance flick down to her case, his expression then for a moment hidden as she sat in a line of sunlight that came into the room, her sight of him as he moved momentarily blinded.

He came nearer, moved out of the ray of sunlight giving her full view of his face that just missed being handsome, though still plenty there in that straight nose and firm mouth that could, if he allowed it, appear to have a generous look to it, to appeal to any girl who might be interested—which she wasn't.

'Who are you?' he asked curtly, seeming to have had his fill of giving her the twice-over from dark eyes which she saw held nothing but suspicion, even as she noted that his voice was authoritative just as though he was used to giving orders, used to getting answers pronto. Did she have news for him!

'I might ask you the same question,' she replied, irked by his manner.

That had his eyes narrowing, she observed. He wasn't liking at all that she wasn't telling him one syllable of why she had called, or of why she was sitting taking her ease in the superbly appointed room. But she hadn't come here to be bullied or brow-beaten by anyone. And certainly not by someone who, instinct had her knowing, was as alien as just being there felt to her.

'Mrs Pinder tells me you call yourself Todd,' he said, pushing his hands into the pockets of the fawn slacks that teamed with the summer-weight dark brown shirt he had on.

'Why shouldn't I?' Alandra answered, discovering there was something about the man that nettled her. 'It's my name.'

'You are claiming some sort of kinship with the Todd family?' he enquired, his voice even, where hers had started to have an edge to it.

That was the last thing she was claiming, if the rest of the Todd clan were like her grandfather. Though with some sixth sense telling her that this man wasn't a Todd, she did not feel any inclination to discuss with him who her forebears were.

'You must be a Carstairs,' she said instead, memory trying to recall just what through the years she had gleaned of the set-up at Roseacres.

'That doesn't show very brilliant deduction,' she was informed, his voice gone cold since she was evading all his questions. 'Roseacres has been populated by Carstairs and Todds for more than forty years.'

'You were born here?' she queried, and then that memory she wanted came to her. 'You must be Matt Carstairs.' And her tongue unwary at her not so slow deduction after all, 'I remember my father telling me that even at the age of eleven you were on the way to becoming the same reprobate he was in his teens.'

'Your father?'

The words had come sharply, no acknowledgment there as to whether she had guessed correctly that he was Matt Carstairs, son of the senior partner in the Carstairs and Todd engineering company. She knew though, as he gave her a third hard scrutiny, that his brain was doing a quick flip back.

And as he started to say, 'You're . . .' she knew he had got her filed.

'I'm Edward Todd's daughter,' she said, and did not have to add 'and proud of it' because it was there in the very look of her.

'You can prove this?' was rapped at her before she could think. 'From what I've been told,' she hadn't missed the dark scepticism in his eyes, 'Edward's wife was too frail ever to have children.'

'Then aren't I a lovely surprise,' she retorted—that or be best by tears that her parents had so wanted their union to be complete with family, that her mother had taken that risk by bringing her into the world. 'And yes,' she said snappily, her mind on that dreadful letter she had in her bag, 'yes, I can prove it.'

A mocking note appeared in his voice, that alone telling her that he was still as suspicious as the devil about her. 'You have your birth certificate with you— how thoughtful,' he jibed, rattling her to replying, not liking him or his discrediting mind one little bit:

'I never like to leave anything to chance.'

Which had him pouncing before she could draw another breath, 'Why have you come?'

His question was bluntly put, but what was in his mind was anyone's guess as she saw his eyes flick to her weekend case. At the thought that he might think that she had called for that same handout her grandfather had thought her mother had been after, Alandra went from being merely rattled to growing so angry, that she was having a hard time to contain it.

'That's my business,' she tartly told him.

But she saw then, as without another word he strode to the door as though intending to close it—to shut them in so that he could sort her out—that Matt

Carstairs, if that was who he was, was very definitely going to make it his business. It was there in every line of him, that much was obvious.

But just as he reached the door, someone else had reached it from the hall side. And a white-haired man of average height came and stood in the doorway. He was a thin beaky-looking man, an erect man who looked to be sprightly and nimble—and not at all anyone's idea of an elderly seventy-year-old. He looked tough, too, Alandra saw, and permanently grouchy, no music in his voice as, not having yet seen her, he said:

'Matt, you know that . . .' He spotted her then, and broke off.

And Alandra, looking at him as he came into the room, found that although she had not wanted to allow her grandfather one courtesy, she was getting to her feet.

Silently, she watched and waited as he came closer. And when he stopped and for long seconds stared at her, she saw deep frown lines groove on his forehead. But she had no word to say to him, and he none for her as he turned to the man who, keeping his eyes steady on the two of them, had now moved from his position by the door, and was coming in their direction.

And it was left to Matt Carstairs to introduce the two—the elderly man who still had the gait of a man years younger, and the young woman whose solemn face was giving nothing away of the very low regard in which she held the other.

'This,' said Matt Carstairs, pausing only marginally as if to assess how the older man would take it, 'this woman claims to be your granddaughter, sir—she says she is Edward's child.'

CHAPTER TWO

FOR stunned seconds after Matt Carstairs had announced who she was claiming to be, Alain Todd stared at her as though thunderstruck. And had there been any doubt in her mind that he might somehow have been aware of her existence, then she knew by the very fact of his incredulous look, that it had never so much as entered his head that her father might have had any offspring.

Matt Carstairs was watching them still, she noted, as her grandfather came out of his shock and at last barked, 'Edward's child! You—you're saying you're Edward's child!'

Disbelief was in that voice which, although shaken, was not quavery or weak. And if some impulse in her had her ready to give him a moment because of his years to get over that shock, then the fact that he had recovered and was not about to credit the truth of what he had been told, had her ignoring that instinctive impulse.

'Alandra Todd at your service,' she said, and looked him straight in his faded blue eyes.

'Alandra . . .!'

The exclamation was involuntary on hearing that, for some reason she couldn't fathom, she had been named after him. But her grandfather was recovering fast. What Matt Carstairs thought on hearing her name she could only guess, probably that she was making it up to get an 'in' with the old man. But she wasn't taking any heed of Matt Carstairs, she was here to deal only with the older man who had recovered from hearing her first name just as quickly as he had from learning who she was. And he was

21

showing himself to be every bit as unlovable as she had thought he would be.

'You can prove you are who you say you are?' he questioned abruptly, the disbelief in him blatant.

His disbelief angered her. It made her wonder why she had bothered to come. Then she was brought up short on remembering that she was here because it was what her mother had asked of her.

'Obviously you're delighted to see me,' she said, sarcasm flooding her voice.

'Lucy Porter was not strong enough to have children,' was the sharp answer.

'Well, she had me!' Alandra flared, sparks flashing from her green eyes to hear this man, who had written that awful letter, so much as mention her mother's name.

Her grandfather was as nasty as she had imagined him to be, she thought. And she was not made to feel any better disposed to either of the men in the room when his chin thrust forward at about the same angle as hers, the older man put the same question that Matt Carstairs had asked not many minutes before.

'Why have you come?' he queried contentiously.

'Are you sure *he* isn't your son?' she replied shortly, indicating the tall dark-haired man who had not so far intruded, but looked ready to take over should Alain Todd need his services. 'You're as suspicious as he is.'

But it was at that point that Matt Carstairs did have something to say. For just then a car being driven at full throttle was heard coming up the drive. Alandra heard it, and knew that they had too, when he interrupted to suggest:

'Perhaps your sitting room would be a better place to continue your—discussion.'

'It would be more private,' Alain Todd agreed. And his attention came back to Alandra. 'Come with me,' he said.

Since it seemed likely that whoever had arrived would

soon be another person to take sides against her, although she was certain that she could hold her own against any of them, Alandra thought it a good idea to adjourn to wherever it was that would be more private.

'Lead the way,' she accepted. But found she was briefly delayed when, having forgotten about her case, she discovered that Matt Carstairs had not done so.

'Don't forget this,' he said, mockery there as he picked it up and handed it to her as though to say he wanted no trace of her in the room.

Without thanks, she took it from him and followed in her grandfather's wake to the already open door. At the door she turned, intending to tell Matt Carstairs that three was a crowd, but she saw that she had no need— he had not moved, so clearly he was staying behind to greet whoever it was who had just arrived.

Crossing the hall she entered a room that housed a cosy-looking three-piece suite, bookshelves, a small writing desk and a chair over by the window, and she realised it was what it had been called—it was a private sitting room.

'Take a seat,' grunted Alain Todd when he had the door closed, 'and tell me why I should believe you are who you say you are.'

'Frankly, I don't care whether you believe me or not,' Alandra declared, and didn't. 'And I'll stand if you don't mind—I'm not stopping. I wouldn't have come at all but for my mother asking me to . . .'

'Your mother asked you to come?' he broke in sharply, instant suspicion there that had her hating him for it.

'Contrary to your permanent belief that my mother, my father too, or myself, ever wanted anything from you,' she said, seeing no reason to pull her punches since he was still ready to believe the very worst of her mother, 'my mother did not send me here for a handout.' And unable to resist it, 'The letter you sent under the erroneous impression when my father died that we wanted anything from you, was more than enough to let us know we would rather starve than accept a penny from you.'

'You've seen—that letter?'

Without answering, Alandra dipped into her bag and handed the letter to him. That he did not need to read it, or that he should have instant recall of the letter he had penned, did not surprise her. Apart from its disgraceful contents, it was the only communication they had ever received from him.

But what did surprise her was that not only did his suspicious manner fall from him to have that letter in his hands, but that, as suddenly, the churlishness he had shown her, should drain away too. And it was just as if he was excusing the way he had written, that with his voice halting, he said:

'I was—upset—at the time. It didn't seem right that— that my son should be dead and that the woman everyone thought would not make it past thirty should still be alive.'

She had not expected him to come near to apologising for the way he had written, and that he should appear to regret having done so, chipped a kink into the hate she felt for him. And she almost softened towards him because he must be saying that he disowned his son, but still felt a father's feeling for him.

But that was before she remembered that her mother had been upset too at the time, devastated in fact. And added to her suffering was the letter this sprightly white-haired man had written.

'If you wished my mother dead then—you now have your wish,' she coldly told him. And a vulnerability crept over her, as the loss of her mother was still so recent. 'My mother died a month ago.'

He did not offer her false sympathy, and she was glad that he did not. Yet his voice had mellowed when he reminded her, 'Your mother asked you to come to Roseacres, you said,' adding, 'She meant that you should come to live with us?'

'That she never did,' Alandra denied hotly, aware that her tone had stung any sign of softening out of her grandfather. But, even having no idea of why her mother had wanted her to make this visit, she was objecting strongly that he should think that to make her home at Roseacres had for an instant been in her mother's mind. 'I don't know why she wanted me to come,' she told him flatly, 'but now that my promise to her has been kept, I'll say goodbye.'

She did not offer to shake hands with him. She felt weepy suddenly, and wanted to be gone. Quickly she took up her case and moved to the door.

'Where are you going?'

Her grandfather's voice, returned to being grumpy, caught up with her just as her fingers closed round the door handle. 'Back to where I came from,' she replied, and turned the handle.

'I didn't see your car on the drive.'

Car! They couldn't have afforded a moped! 'I came by train. There's a return one at six,' she said, making to open the door.

'Not on Saturday, there isn't.'

Alandra spun round, her turn to discredit her hearing. 'The six o'clock to London—doesn't run on Saturdays!' she gasped, her hand leaving the door in her amazement. 'But the taxi-driver said . . .'

'If it was Jim Lasky, his head is so full of his dahlias he wouldn't know a Saturday from a Monday,' her grandfather supplied, seeming to her mind to be spitefully pleased she had been given wrong information, as he added, 'There's not another train back to London today.'

Staring at him coldly, she hid her dismay as best she could. Wasn't it just like the man she had thought him that he should take such small-minded delight that she appeared stranded.

'Goodbye,' she said stonily, and turned once more for the door.

'I've just told you,' came her grandfather's voice again, 'there isn't another train out of Ferny Druffield today.'

'I heard you,' she said, half turning. 'But even in this benighted spot there must be someone in the village who will take in a stranded passenger overnight.'

'You wouldn't do that to me?' his question came as her hand went once more to the door handle.

'Do what to you?' she asked, frowning in annoyance that he was delaying her when she had a three-mile walk in front of her, hopeful as she was that the village had a police house where she could go and make enquiries regarding overnight accommodation.

'The Todd name is highly respected in the village,' Alain Todd told her proudly, 'but villagers talk.' And, sneakily, she thought, 'I can see you have inherited your father's pride—won't you allow me my pride? I don't want gossip rife that I refused my son Edward's daughter shelter for the night. Everyone knows we have rooms to spare here.'

'You're suggesting I stay the night *here*!'

'Is it so unthinkable?' he questioned shortly.

'Yes it is,' she smartly said back.

'You'd be doing what your father would never have done,' he told her craftily. 'No matter how often or how violently we quarrelled, he would never let the village have a whisper of it. *He* never asked anyone in the village to put *him* up overnight.'

Another chink appeared in Alandra's armour as she looked at the deadpan expression on the face of the man she had sworn to hate. And she was pulled two ways, memory there of her father, the way he had been. Happy-go-lucky, laughing, seldom did he allow her to see him down, and proud, oh so very proud. She didn't want to stay so much as a minute more under this hostile roof—and yet, would her father have wanted that she stayed the night in the village? Would her mother have wanted that?

She hesitated, and wanted to be gone. But something stronger than herself was tugging at her. Ungraciously, she gave in.

'Very well,' she said coldly.

Her grandfather's grace was no improvement on hers she saw, when, without looking in the slightest bit pleased to have got her agreement, he brushed her out of the way of the door and opened it.

My God! she thought, what a pair of lungs he's got on him, as no thought in his head to ring the bell which she noted at the side of the fireplace, he stood at the door and bellowed:

'Mrs Pinder!'

Up in the room to which the housekeeper had taken her after coming in and beaming on being introduced to Mr Todd's granddaughter, Alandra had long since regretted giving in to her wily grandfather. She could have found someone in the village to put her up for the night, she was sure of it. Why she should let that crafty old fox put one over on her was a mystery to her. She had come here ready to hate him and, she admitted, had found little to like in him on having met the old devil. But yet here she was, to her mind having put up very little resistance, ensconced in a bedroom that was the height of luxury with its *en suite* bathroom, and having given her word to stay until morning.

One thing was for certain, though, she thought with self-disgust as she took her overnight things from her case—she was catching the first train out in the morning. She went and had a bath knowing that since the only dress she had with her was the one she had worn all day, it was going to be that one she would have to go down to dinner in, and wondering if something as basic as the fact that she shared the same blood as Alain Todd had anything to do with her agreeing to stay without much of a fight.

She came from the pink-and-white bathroom, determined then that if she had shown a certain weakness in character in giving in to the cunning of the seventy-year-old who was too sharp ever to turn into a sweet old man, then she would show him at dinner that she wasn't there because she wanted to be there.

At five to eight, dinner was at eight so Mrs Pinder had informed her, freshened from her bath, Alandra took one last look at her image, and left her room wondering who else would be at the table.

Would the non-smiling Matt Carstairs be there? Perhaps his wife too. Maybe children of his—he looked virile enough to have a whole parcel of them. She realised then that if other people were to be present at dinner—maybe she would meet her aunt Eunice and her cousin Robert—and as her quarrel was with none save her grandfather, and maybe, since he seemed tarred with the same brush, Matt Carstairs, then the good manners her mother had set so much store by meant that she said nothing that might make the rest of them feel uncomfortable.

Reaching the bottom of the stairs, she made for the only downstairs room she knew other than her grandfather's sitting room. The drawing room door was closed, giving her the feeling that if she was expected to find for herself where in the house everyone assembled, then she was not expected with welcome.

She opened the door, the feeling that she was not welcome magnified when not one of the people in the 'pre-dinner drink-in-hand' group made any move to come towards her, or to acknowledge her in any way.

She was on the point of thinking, damn the whole lot of them, she wasn't hungry anyway, when her grandfather, having made some comment to Matt Carstairs, detached himself from the three people he was standing with, and came over to where she was standing.

'Come and meet your cousins,' he said, his face as unsmiling as hers.

Curiosity stirred, negating the mutiny of her

thoughts. Cousins! She had known about Cousin Robert, but ... Having no axe to grind with her Aunt Eunice's children, Alandra went forward, prepared to be pleasant to her cousins even if she wasn't so prepared to be pleasant to the two more mature men in the room.

'You know Matt, of course,' said her grandfather as Matt Carstairs, as unsmiling as the rest of them, flicked her a glance from dark suspicious eyes.

She flicked back a glance of her own, and then ignored him. She turned then to be introduced to her cousins. The slim blonde girl was about her own age, she thought, the man standing next to her about her own five feet nine inches in height, but with such a wild crop of straw-coloured hair, she couldn't help but think that even Worzel Gummidge wouldn't want it for second-best.

But if she was ready to be pleasant, friendly even, to her cousins since she had no quarrel with them, she was soon to discover that her cousins were not the least interested in returning the compliment.

Robert, so she had been right about his name, did bring himself to shake hands, and did manage to mumble, 'Hello.' But all her cousin Josephine gave in acknowledging she had a cousin she had never known about, was an affected small tweak of the corners of her mouth, giving Alandra a feeling that had her grandfather not been there, then she wouldn't have received even that much.

Taken aback by such rudeness, she saw Josephine, without addressing one word to her, turn away and go over to Matt, where, laying a possessive hand on his arm as if staking claim, she batted her blue eyes at him, and cooed:

'Matt, you'll simply have to tell me all about the porcelain fair you and Grandfather went to today.'

She's welcome to him, Alandra thought, wondering, since there wasn't a Mrs Matt Carstairs in evidence, if the ill-mannered Josephine and the hostile Matt Carstairs were engaged, for all the girl's left hand was ringless.

'There's nothing to tell, poppet,' she heard Matt reply, the answer there in the way he spoke to her cousin showing that whatever she felt about him, to him she was still the youngster who had happened to grow up in the same house. But it was as his eyes moved from Josephine to look straight at her, and he added, 'The piece Alain thought was genuine turned out to be phoney on closer inspection,' that Alandra felt her hackles begin to rise.

The swine! she thought. She had no idea what her grandfather had told him of what had gone on in his private sitting room, but it was just as if he was saying that she might have pulled the wool over the old man's eyes, but that he had seen through her.

And Alandra found herself in a 'for two pins' situation. Either she could charge up to her room, collect her case and storm the three miles to the village—away from this cold house where if anybody smiled the unusual sound of cracking faces would echo like cannoning thunder—or she could stay and declare war on the lot of them.

Mrs Pinder coming in, Matt casually removing Josephine's tentacles from his arm and saying a general, 'Shall we go into dinner,' had the decision made for her. And Alandra felt so damn mad at not just him, but all of them; her female cousin whom she had just caught giving a snobby look to her inferior linen dress that was denying its 'crease resistant' label; her male cousin, who wasn't a man at all if the way he looked to be frightened to death of her grandfather was anything to go by; and last of all, her grandfather, who, when she had been all set to hate him, had proved such a wily old fox as to have her agreeing to stay overnight, when she would have shuddered at the very idea had anyone suggested it before her coming here.

As her anger boiled over, and her father's pride which she had inherited was up in arms, Alandra decided that it was about time war was declared. She was furious enough then to give them all something to think about.

'Come along, Grandfather,' she said warmly, the word 'grandfather' leaving her for the first time, and there was a gladness in her that she had been able to bring it out without it sticking in her throat. 'You can show me where in this vast house the dining room is.'

She then did a little arm-clinging of her own, as catching hold of his arm, she hung on to it as they all trooped out into the hall, not missing the three pairs of hostile eyes which were witnessing her every action.

Oh, roll on tomorrow when she could get out of here, she thought, hers the only smile in the dining room when, as if he had just remembered such old world courtesies, her grandfather pulled out a chair for her at the beautiful, highly polished table.

Her grandfather sat one end, Matt Carstairs, she noted, sat the other. The table, she thought, would be massive if fully extended. But since there were only five of them, it was left so that there was about two feet of room between each place setting.

'You live here with Grandfather?' Alandra addressed Josephine seated opposite her, taking the battle straight into the enemy camp as Mrs Pinder finished serving the first course of avocado vinaigrette.

She thought for a moment that her cousin was going to ignore her. Then she observed Josephine catch the frowning glance of her grandparent. 'Yes,' she muttered.

Alandra smiled a smile she hoped only she knew was false. She then looked at her cousin Robert to the right of her, but since he was tucking into his avocado as if eating was fast going out of style, and since he hadn't been so openly hostile as his sister, she decided that she would do better to concentrate on the girl.

'Do your parents still live here, too?' she went on to ask.

'Your cousins' parents were divorced some years ago,' answered Matt Carstairs for Josephine.

'I'm sorry.' Her apology was automatic, a sensitivity there that had her intention to send them all up, if she had half a chance, vanishing. But only for a moment—they still had their parents. 'You must forgive me,' she went on. 'There is so much that I don't know about *my* family.'

And not a lot she cared to know, she thought, thinking that her parents might have been hard up more times than enough, but never could she remember, when her mother had been well enough to join them for meals, that they had ever eaten in such a gloomy atmosphere. Her cousins might be looking down at her as the poor relation, but she had had something they had never had by the look of them—a happy childhood.

'Your mother,' she addressed Josephine again as Mrs Pinder cleared the first course and brought in serving dishes so they could help themselves, 'my aunt Eunice,' she said, throwing in the possessive pronoun for the sheer hell of it, 'is she well?'

'Eunice married again,' that grumpily from her grandfather. 'We don't see her very often.'

'You mean she could bear to leave . . .' she motioned with her hands, '. . . all this?' A cold silence greeted her. 'Love is a very powerful emotion, isn't it?' she murmured.

'You know anything about the emotion?'

The challenge had come from Matt Carstairs, and she looked down the table at him. Too clearly he thought her remark, her barely hidden meaning that her father hadn't thought twice about leaving and calling for his love en route, a bit near too being hurtful.

'Do you?' she answered, and determined not to be sat on, 'Are you married, Matt?'

'No, he isn't.'

What a family they were for answering for each other, Alandra thought, but at least Josephine had come away from being monosyllabic, just, to reply for Matt. Though she was certain that he was more than able to make his own replies. She forced another smile at her cousin.

'You'll have to see what you can do to get him hooked up—with a friend,' she added as if it was a hasty afterthought. And then added confidingly, 'Men start to get a little crusty if they're left to be a bachelor for too long, don't they?' And not stopping to see who was choking on what, she turned her attention to Robert who, she noticed, was looking at her as though mesmerised.

'You'll have finished at university now, Robert, I daresay. What sort of work do you do for a living?' That hair! she thought, as he looked at her speechlessly, really with all their money you would think somebody would take him to a decent barber. Matt's hair now, although it looked as though it would have waved if allowed, looked to be expertly cut. 'You do work, I suppose?'

'Do you?' Words she had used were bounced back.

Again Alandra looked to the end of the table. She had thought she was ready to bat off any of Matt Carstairs' questions, but memory of why she was at present without a job had her hesitating.

'Not—at present,' she said shortly, striving against sudden unexpected tears that would catch her out at the least expected moment and had done ever since the day of her mother's funeral when she had broken down and cried her heart out.

Josephine, her tongue loosened, came in to give her the stiffening she needed. Though there had been no need for her to home in and range herself on Matt's side. Because, from his cold look, she gleaned it was no more than he expected that she was one of the world's layabouts, and he looked to have finished with his attack.

'What sort of work *do* you do—er—when you are working?' Josephine enquired in that superior tone that made Alandra wish she had got more time to cut her down to size.

'Secretarial, actually,' she said, leaving out the dogs-body part.

'Oh,' said Josephine, looking stumped for a moment. 'You went to secretarial college?'

Alandra studied her for some moments. The hesitation in Josephine's voice had given her the impression that the bitchiness in her was not a natural part of her cousin's nature.

But a quick glance round the table, no other conversation going on, told her that everybody was waiting for what she had to say. Her grandfather, unsmiling still, was having a rest from the steak he had been cutting into, Robert was still looking at her with that mesmerised look that gave her an added impression that he rarely contributed to meal-time conversation, and Matt Carstairs—she wasn't quite sure how he was looking, save that he was still so suspicious of her he wasn't going to believe a word she said anyway.

'Of course,' she said, 'you know as little about me as I know about you.' She smiled generally about, then beamed her smile particularly in her grandfather's direction. 'For a start, you'll probably be relieved to know that I have given Grandfather proof that I am who I say I am,' and while eyes went to him, she added, 'haven't I, dear?' Her grandfather looked pop-eyed to hear anyone call him 'dear', and Robert and Josephine looked goggle-eyed, too, that the acerbic old man should be referred to as 'dear' by anyone, and Alandra, enjoying herself immensley, almost giggled.

'That's between you and me, and no one else,' the old man recovered himself to say shortly.

Abruptly the feeling of wanting to giggle left her. Quite plainly, he was telling her that no one was to know about that letter she had returned to him. Well, serve him right, he should be ashamed, she thought. But though still ready to oppose him given the chance, for once she found herself not too unwilling to go along with him.

There was a pause as Mrs Pinder came in with the dessert. And by the time she had gone out again, Alandra had grown tired of the baiting game she had instigated. From the way her two cousins had their eyes on her, however, it was apparent that they had recovered from hearing their grandfather being called 'dear' and were waiting to find out still more about her.

'Actually, I never did get to secretarial school,' she said, digging in her heels. 'My father—Ned he was known as by everyone,' she inserted with another artificial smile at her grandfather since he apparently had never been able to bring himself to call his son anything other than Edward, a starchy name that just didn't fit the laughing-eyed man she remembered, 'died when I was fourteen. So naturally since we were nearly always broke, I left school at sixteen and received my secretarial tuition at evening classes.'

She thought she had managed to bring that out quite lightly, as though that tuition had been a game to her and not as deadly earnest and important as it had been. Nothing there in her voice, she thought, to reveal how she had raced to her classes and raced back home again.

'I don't suppose you ever cut any of those classes?' Matt Carstairs had joined in, sounding, she thought, as though, while he might commend any girl for getting her education the best way she could afford, in his view she had joined the college purely for the social activities that might be found.

'Often,' she replied, giving him the benefit of a pleasant smile. *He* was the last person she would have told how, when her mother looked too peaky to be left on her own, she had cut a class and in consequence had to swot like mad to catch up.

He saw through her phoney smile of course, she knew that, but her answer seemed to satisfy him. Oh, to have time to sort her grandfather out, and then to start on him—not to mention her two delightful cousins.

'Where do—did you live?' Robert, at long last coming out from his mesmerised state, had decided to join in the conversation.

'London,' she told him, 'though not always in the same place.'

'You moved around a lot?' This question from the blonde across from her.

'That's right,' Alandra replied. But she didn't trust her cousin's look, and was not totally surprised when the barely concealed barb came.

'I've heard of people doing that,' she said thoughtfully, and while Alandra was expecting the dart to be in connection with gypsies, she was taken aback, but only for a moment, to hear her add, 'Isn't that what they call living on one's wits?'

For perhaps two seconds, Alandra stared down at the last small spoonful of crème caramel on her plate. A hush had fallen on the room with no one coming in to make any comment. Not that she expected them to. She rather thought her performance this far had shown that she was more than equal to dealing with her uppity cousin without the need of help from anyone.

Daintily, she spooned the last of the caramel into her mouth. Elegantly, she disposed of it. Then, unhurriedly, she stood to her feet. And pleasantly she looked at the blue-eyed, and to her mind, empty-headed, snobby blonde.

'Cousin dear,' she said softly. 'Don't you think that if it falls on only one of Grandfather's female descendants to be favoured with any wit at all—it is then incumbent upon that *one* female to use it?'

She did not bother to say goodnight to any of them.

She was aware as she sailed loftily out from the dining room that one or two chairs had scraped back, as if the courtesy had been afforded her of one or two males among them rising to their feet. But she had no idea whatsoever which one of them had braved the sky falling in and had emitted that short bark of a laugh at her parting shot—she didn't think she much cared who it was.

CHAPTER THREE

ALANDRA'S thoughts when she got out of bed the next
morning were many, and varied. Her father, she
reasoned, a man with an ability to see the funny side of
most things must, during his many years of living at
Roseacres, have often laughed. Yet recalling that
dreadful hour or so, give or take five minutes, spent at
dinner last night with her equally dreadful cousins, her
permanently disgruntled grandfather, and that awful
Matt Carstairs, she couldn't help but wonder if even her
father's irrepressible good humour would have surfaced.

There had been the sound of *one* laugh last night, she
remembered. And she rather thought that laugh
following her intimation that she considered her cousin
witless had come from Matt Carstairs. Though why he
had laughed she was still trying to fathom as she
showered and pulled on jeans and a shirt. Just as last
night she had puzzled at the alien sound in the cold
cheerless house.

It couldn't be that, unexpectedly, she had amused
him, she pondered, going over to her bedroom window
and staring out at the truly magnificent view of rolling
acres of fields and pasture land. He was clever was Matt
Carstairs, she didn't doubt that, but she was still
tugging over why, when he, like the rest of them, was
humourless to the point of being a pain, he should
suddenly laugh.

A few minutes later, certain his laugh had not been
from amusement, Alandra decided to forget Matt
Carstairs. It was early still, but she had some enquiries
to make about a train back to London. She left her
room thinking she had better go and investigate for
some signs of life.

Negotiating the stairs, she paused at the bottom, her eyes appreciating a Sèvres vase that stood on an antique chest in the hall, the idea lighting down of how her father had not thought twice about giving up his right to handle such beautiful objects when, temper flying, he had left his home and his inheritance.

A smile hovered, about to break as she thought of her father and his love for her mother. But that smile didn't make it. For suddenly she was stopped dead in her tracks as another thought touched down. And all at once she knew just exactly why everyone had been so 'anti' her last night. Quite suddenly she had the answer to just why Matt Carstairs had laughed so unexpectedly.

Amazed that she hadn't thought of it before, Alandra saw then why her cousins, Matt Carstairs, the three of them, were against her! They thought, must do since they knew nothing of her promise to her mother, that her only reason for being there was to see what chance she had of claiming some sort of an inheritance!

'Good morning, Miss Todd.'

Alandra came away from her astounded thoughts to see that Mrs Pinder had appeared as if from nowhere while she had been too staggered from her deductions to have noticed her.

'Oh—Good morning Mrs Pinder,' she replied, of necessity having to leave her astonishing realisation for the moment.

'If you're looking for the breakfast room,' the housekeeper suggested, 'it's this way.'

She hadn't been looking for the breakfast room, but Alandra fell into step beside the housekeeper, thinking that in the absence of anything stronger to restore her, a cup of coffee would go down very nicely.

The breakfast room was empty, but with Mrs Pinder fussing over her, Alandra took a fifth chair that had been pulled up to the table, and had to hold back on thoughts that wanted to tear in. And, declining anything more than a piece of toast, it was not until the housekeeper had departed that she had time to get her thoughts into any sort of order.

But thoughts that were fighting for precedence were again temporarily shelved as, glancing around the room with its beautiful carved sideboard, Alandra's eyes caught movement outside the French doors. And it was there that she observed, lost to anything but the magnificence of a delightful rose garden, her grandfather.

So he was an early riser too! Well, she hoped he would stay where he was for a while. She was in no mood for his grumpy countenance this morning, she had urgent thoughts to deal with.

It was all so obvious now, she mused, as her eyes left her grandfather. She couldn't understand why it had taken so long for everything to fall into place. Though perhaps it wasn't so surprising since, never having had any money to speak of, thoughts of gaining that commodity without having to work for it had never visited her.

But she made herself think of it then as she tried to see the picture as her cousins and Matt Carstairs must see it. They thought, she was now positive, that she had come there to set about claiming a third share—or was it a half since her father should have been entitled to half—of her grandfather's estate!

He couldn't last for ever, she knew, just as she knew that even a tiny share in the Carstairs and Todd combine must be worth a bomb. But little did any of them know that she wouldn't touch a penny of her grandfather's money.

Her mind going back over the previous evening, she dubbed them a miserable bunch, and decided that if that was what having money did to you, then thank goodness she didn't have any.

Matt Carstairs' laugh made sense now. It was not that she had unexpectedly amused him by her comment that if one had wit one should use it. She had already revealed that she and her parents had invariably been hard up, and, waiting throughout that meal for her to slip up, he, she now saw, had taken her comment as proof that she was there to outwit them if she could and take her share of what should have been her father's inheritance.

Anger started to bite. Oh, wouldn't she just love to stay around and give them all a few moments of heart failure. Oh, wouldn't she just love to ... Her thoughts broke off as the door opened and Mrs Pinder bearing a pot of coffee came in followed by Matt Carstairs who had opened the door for her.

Alandra had a few moments to control a surge of dislike in her heart for Matt Carstairs and his suspicious mind as Mrs Pinder, apparently already knowing he always ate bacon and egg at this time of the day, went out saying she would be along with his breakfast shortly.

But he would never know what it cost her as casually, while he took a chair at the table, Alandra reached for the coffee pot and said cheerfully, 'Good morning, Matt,' while resisting the temptation to empty the scalding contents over his head. 'Black or white?'

She was to gather from his taciturn response of a grunted, 'Black,' that either he did not feel like laughing this morning, or that it was unheard of for anyone to be cheerful in this house not only this early, for it couldn't yet be eight o'clock, but at any time of the day.

Used to pouring coffee and doing all manner of domestic chores, deftly she poured him a cup of black coffee. She nearly choked on refraining from asking him if he would like the whole contents of the sugar bowl emptied into it, but instead placed the bowl down by his right hand. Though she just could not keep back the treacly comment of:

'Do you think an Alka-Seltzer might help?' Nor the wide-eyed innocent remark, 'I have heard it said that they are invaluable when one feels liverish.'

Thunder in the air, she thought, as he frowned darkly at her. And she heard that it was just too much for his black soul to take to have someone as bright as her sitting with him at breakfast.

'How long are you staying?' he questioned, not short on asperity, she noticed.

The impulse to tell him 'for a whole month' just to see his reaction, was almost insurmountable. But on catching the look in his eyes that told her that wouldn't have surprised him since he knew damn well why she was there, Alandra lost the impulse, and some of her control went with it.

'The whole damned lot of you can stay miserable on your own,' she said with some heat. 'I'm catching the first train back to London this morning.'

'What—so soon?' he replied, and his look was steady on her as slowly he drawled, his disbelief evident, 'Surely you're not leaving before you have what you came for?'

'What I came . . .?'

She knew a moment's confusion before his meaning became clear. Then she felt some small shock that he was not dressing it up, but was coming out into the open to show her how very accurate her thoughts had been. And it was at that moment that the gloves came off.

'Oh,' she murmured airily, 'you mean that part of the inheritance my dear cousins think I'm here to put in my claim for?' And managing a thoughtful smile in the face of her suppositions being proved true, since he wasn't arguing, 'Now isn't that an idea?' she added as though giving the matter serious thought.

'Not, I'm afraid,' Matt Carstairs answered, a mocking note there, his eyes still watchful, 'a very good one.'

Alandra tilted her head slightly to one side as she threw him an enquiring glance. But she was as mocking as he as she trotted out the only thing she thought he could be meaning.

'You're not telling me,' she said with an affected gasp, 'that he's gone and willed everything to the local dog and cat home?' Starting to enjoy herself, painfully she said, 'He wouldn't do—that—would he!'

With an elbow propped on the table, a masculine finger rubbing his chin, Matt Carstairs looked as though he had all the answers as he considered her question. And it was with a smile that was as thoughtfully false as hers had been that he told her:

'He might—if he had anything to leave.'

Involuntarily her green eyes widened. Carstairs and Todd were a leading company, they couldn't be broke! It was impossible! She knew it was impossible and it annoyed her mightily that he should try to make her believe the firm was bankrupt purely so she would forget about any claim—especially since she wasn't interested in their wretched finances anyway.

'You're trying to tell me that the firm of Carstairs and Todd are on their uppers?' she said stonily, her disbelief evident.

'The firm is expanding rapidly,' he baffled her by replying.

'Then why . . .?' She didn't get to finish the question. For he was butting in, his mocking note gone as levelly he eyed her, and said:

'The only problem—as far as you are concerned that is—is that, while I see no reason to change the name of the Company, your grandfather no longer has a share in it.'

Alandra stared at him, her look more disbelieving than ever. 'You're saying . . .'

'I'm saying that your grandfather has sold his share to me.'

'You . . .' She broke off. It didn't make sense. Robert's name wasn't Todd, but surely her grandfather would never have sold away his grandson's right to be part of the firm—would he?

Her eyes flicked past Matt and out to where her

grandfather was still snipping away occasionally at the roses. And she remembered then the way, because her father, his son, would not toe the line and stay in the business; the way, because her father had married someone her grandfather considered totally unsuitable—though there had been rows before that, often—her grandfather had disowned him. And in remembering, she knew that, oh yes, he would sell out if it suited him. He was ruthless was her grandfather, she didn't have to think past that dreadful letter he had sent to her mother at a time when she had been heart-broken, to know that, even if he had excused it by saying that he had been upset too.

Her eyes left the French doors, and she looked at the man opposite her. A man, she realised, who had been watching her as if reading her every thought. A man, who, she suddenly knew with an inner conviction, could be every bit as ruthless as her grandfather if it suited him.

'Got it?' he enquired cynically, as if having watched her weigh everything up for herself, he knew that she had indeed 'Got it'.

'You own Carstairs and Todd,' she said, no question there, but a statement of fact.

'Are you now going to pretend that you didn't know?'

'About your take-over, you mean?' she enquired, genuinely puzzled. But she was again faced with mockery, as with not an atom of belief in his face, he said:

'You didn't waste any time in getting here, did you?'

In actual fact it had been weeks before she had acted on that promise she had made. But since he did not know about that promise, she had to confess that she hadn't a clue what he was talking about.

'I don't understand,' she said. And saw neither mockery, nor anything else but hard aggression in him when he rapped:

'Like hell you don't—my taking sole charge of the company made headlines in all the nationals on Friday.'

Her own aggression rose at his tone. But it was dimmed as she realised that with her arriving the very day after that announcement had appeared in the press, to anyone with his suspicious turn of mind, it would look far more than just coincidence that her grandfather should be paid out what must be a colossal sum one day, and that she should turn up out of the blue the very next day.

Rousing herself above caring what the suspicious-minded Matt Carstairs should think anyway, there was a fair degree of sarcasm in her voice as she addressed the man she considered an arrogant, know-it-all male, and pleasantly, she said:

'Forgive my ignorance, but if my grandfather has sold out his half of a mammoth concern such as Carstairs and Todd, then would it be foolish of me to imagine that he came out of the deal very nicely?'

'It would appear that way, wouldn't it,' Matt agreed with a pleasantness that was as phoney as her own. 'But unfortunately for you,' he went on, an edge coming to his voice, 'what the press did not say, because they didn't know, was that the transaction in money terms took place some years ago when your grandfather needed all the money he could lay his hands on to settle with some creditors. The transaction finalised on Friday was a paper one only.'

For long, long moments, Alandra was silent as it came to her to wonder, if, though no mention had been made of how long ago it was when money had changed hands, her mother's letter had reached Roseacres at just a time when to hear Matt Carstairs talk, her grandfather had been on his beam ends. Wouldn't the Todd pride in the old man have had him writing that he had no intention of giving the smallest financial support, simply because he hadn't got it—purely because at that time he had needed every penny he could scrape together?

Suddenly realising that she was actually looking for excuses for that letter, when nothing should excuse what her grandfather had written, she mentally shook herself, and looked up to see that Matt was watching her with a hawk-like intensity. It was just as though, she thought, in the absence of being able to read her mind, he reckoned he had come close by deciding that she was mulling over the set-back to her plans because her grandfather didn't have any money to leave anybody.

'So,' she said thoughtfully, 'my grandfather isn't the wealthy man I thought he was.'

'How does that grab you?' he questioned, his lofty insolent manner taking her Todd pride shooting to the surface.

She counted a silent one to ten, her look considering as her long lashes parted and she studied the strong face in front of her, from his dark hair with its stray flecks of white, his high forehead, past eyes that unflinchingly looked back, down to a chin that said he could be thoroughly obstinate, determined, and unyielding. And then she smiled.

'It could be, Matt dear,' she said, her mouth parting as the devil in her nudged her to bring out that same mischievous endearment she had last night used on her grandfather, 'that I have been making up to totally the wrong man.'

His response was immediate, and angry. She hadn't expected any other. Though it was so abrupt that her words didn't even have time to fade in the hostile air, before he was roughly ramming at her, his chin again thrust aggressively forward.

'Don't try it,' he snarled. And his eyes glinting dangerously, he rapped, 'You may in the past have received certain success from batting those overlong lashes in a male direction, but just don't try it with me.'

And he looked so threatening, so menacing as his

hand on the table bunched into a fist, that for a few seconds her pride deserted her, and she definitely felt scared as he thundered warningly:

'No wide-eyed female with the scent of money in her nostrils is ever likely to turn me over!'

Luckily at that point, Alandra heard Mrs Pinder at the door. And since she was nearest, she was quickly on her feet and going to open it. Her fear receding to see the tray-bearing housekeeper there—he couldn't very well fracture her jaw with that great fist with Mrs Pinder there—though she wouldn't have put it past him.

The girl she thought she was surfaced as Mrs Pinder's body was bent over the table, a buffer between them if she needed one as the plate of bacon and eggs was put before him.

'Was it something I said?' she murmured.

But if he made any reply, she didn't hear it, for her grandfather had stepped through the French doors, and was grunting something to Mrs Pinder to the effect that he would have his breakfast, too.

Her grandfather took his place at the table, but had neither word nor look to spare for her or Matt. Tarred with the same brush, she thought again, for Matt Carstairs hadn't bothered with a good morning to her, either.

And on top again, although not because she no longer had Matt for sole company she was sure, Alandra could not restrain the chirruped, 'Good morning, Grandfather,' that left her, not seeing any excuse for bad manners from either of them, regardless if they had gone on in this same uncivil breakfast way for years.

Alain Todd's surprised look, and the grunt she received for her trouble, were not, she thought, good enough.

'And yes, thank you, Grandfather,' she continued brightly, 'I slept really beautifully.'

Their eyes met, nothing but innocence in green eyes as she stared back at her grim-faced grandparent. She had a distinct impression then that neither of his other grandchildren had ever stood up to him in their lives.

'Less of the sauce from you, young woman,' he grunted as he took his serviette from its silver ring.

But Alandra, still looking at him, did not miss, begrudging though it was, a minute movement at the corners of his mouth. It wasn't quite a twitch but could it be that she had prodded his sense of humour?

'Yes, Grandfather,' she replied with false meekness, but her feeling of cheerfulness suddenly genuine, 'You won't have to put up with me and my sauce for much longer.'

She had his attention she saw as, his serviette falling on to his lap, he frowningly looked at her. And that imp of mischief was riding her again, as she trotted out:

'As soon as I have kissed you goodbye, I shall be on my way.'

Mischief faded as his frown deepened. His look gave her the oddest feeling that it had been years since anyone had kissed him. Not that she could blame them, it must be similar to sucking a lemon, she thought. But, oddly, a feeling akin to being sorry for him smote her—when she didn't want to feel sorry for him. He had made his own bed, let him lie on it, she thought, trying to oust the peculiar idea that she should feel in any way sorry for him.

'Where do you think you're going?' he questioned shortly, taking her a little by surprise because for all his advancing years, he was as sharp as a tack, and could not have forgotten that she was returning to London today. She remembered how wily, how cunning, she had thought him, and whether he considered she was being saucy or not just then, she thought that to be saucy was the best way to deal with his sudden pretence of amnesia, whatever crafty notions might be going through his mind.

'As soundly as I slept last night,' she said lightly, 'as I've just told Matt here, tonight will see me back in my own bed.'

'You're leaving!' he exclaimed, seeming to be taken aback, when he knew very well, she thought, that as far as she was concerned, just one night under his roof was one too many.

'Catching the first Wells Fargo out of here,' she replied, her senses alert at the—was it a smug look?—he exchanged with Matt, as just at that moment Mrs Pinder came in with fresh coffee and her grandfather's porridge.

Having acquainted him with what he already knew anyway, Alandra poured her grandfather a cup, and herself a second cup. And, because she hoped she was above being petty-minded, observing that Matt's cup was empty, she poured him a cup too.

But, she thought, as she raised her cup to her mouth, either she was highly sensitive, or surely, the atmosphere had changed! She took a sip of coffee, then carefully placing her cup in her saucer, she looked across at Matt Carstairs. His expression, she saw, was bland. He was giving nothing away as his eyes met hers. But, she looked quickly at her grandfather, something was going on between the two of them, she knew it, felt it. Even when there had been no verbal communication between the two—they had communicated.

'What . . .' she started to say, her voice sharp.

'If,' interrupted her grandfather, his look as bland as that of the owner of Carstairs and Todd, 'you intend to go back to London today, then I think it only fair to warn you that you might have an awfully long wait for a train.' And while she stared uncomprehendingly at what she was sure now was a twitch to his mouth, he added, 'Matt must have forgotten to tell you—there isn't a train out of Ferny Druffield on Sundays.'

. Her manners, Alandra had to admit later, were no better than theirs, but she wasn't thinking of manners then. She knew damn well that Matt Carstairs had not forgotten about the trains not running on Sundays, and that he had not enlightened her was purely because from where he was sitting, he was sure she hadn't been meaning to leave anyway. Abruptly she stood up, her look serving to kill the two of them as angrily she tossed her serviette down upon the table, and without a word she left the room.

Later that day, her anger cooled, but dislike for all at Roseacres, except maybe Mrs Pinder, in her heart, she was glad of the toast she had eaten at breakfast. It was mid-afternoon when pangs of hunger attacked, for having left the house in fury, she had not returned at lunch time.

She would have to return to Roseacres, she knew that. Just as she knew she would have to spend another night under her grandfather's roof. Though she had been sorely tempted when she had first stormed out of the house, to head downhill for the village to try and find a bed there.

Emotional blackmail, she thought mutinously, when at five o'clock she was tired from her many hours of walking over the beautiful landscape, the hills and valleys her father must have known. Though how could it be through emotional blackmail that she was staying another night? she pondered. Emotional blackmail would have to mean that she felt some sort of affection for that cynical old man, and that was very far from the truth.

She encountered no one in the hall as she went in, though the couple of cars parked on the drive said that someone was at home. She went straight up to her room and thought again that had she been disposed to ask anyone in this household for a favour, she could easily have asked one of them to take her to a railway station where trains did run on Sundays.

Knowing this lot, though, they would probably refuse, she thought as she entered her room. And that would not have done her pride the least bit of good, she mused, flinging herself down on the bed, where she intended to stay until it was time to get changed to go down to dinner. She was glad she hadn't demeaned herself to ask for a favour, only to have her request turned down.

Her dress was certainly earning its keep, she thought ruefully, when at two minutes to eight she was bathed and changed and ready to go downstairs.

Everyone was assembled when she pushed open the drawing room door. She felt all eyes turn to her, but it was Josephine she noticed in particular, her stunning dress making her more than ever aware of the creases in her linen.

'We're just about to go in to dinner, but if you'd like a drink first?' suggested Matt, apparently possessing more manners than she had credited him with, as he separated himself from the group.

His action, the only one of the four of them to acknowledge her presence, since Robert was examining his toe-caps and Josephine was talking to her grandfather, had the instant light of battle that had come to Alandra's eyes dimming.

'No thanks,' she replied quietly. And finding a hint of rebellion because she knew she had to be on her guard for any knife-edged remarks hiding behind that hint of charm Matt was civilly sending her way, 'I wouldn't dream of letting any of you start with cold soup.'

It was Josephine who clung on to her grandfather's arm as they all trooped into the dining room. And if she was saying, 'He's *my* grandfather' then Alandra could smile and let her get on with it. She had had her fill of the Todds, and the one Carstairs too, for that matter. The only reason she had come down to dinner at all was for the simple reason that she was starving.

So hungry was she that she was in no mind to bait any of them this evening, but daintily she ate her way through her meal leaving what talk there was to the others.

It was in this way that she learned that in each other's company Josephine was shortened to Jo, and Robert—Alandra still hadn't got used to his hair—was Robbie. Though, and the thought made her smile, nobody ever lengthened Matt's name to Matthew.

She was idly wondering if perhaps he wasn't Matthew, but had been named just plain Matt, when from the other end of the table she realised that not only had he been watching her, but that he was addressing her too.

'You were smiling a moment ago, Alandra. You were having pleasant thoughts, perhaps?'

There had to be a knife-edge in there somewhere she thought, totally wary of him. 'I was just thinking of the lovely day I have spent today,' she lied, refraining from adding 'outside'. Matt was nobody's fool, no need to underline that 'inside' was murder.

'You've been tramping the hills?'

She threw him a suspicious look. Then she decided to take his remark at face value. Though with the opinion she knew he had of her, she wouldn't have been at all surprised if there wasn't a double entendre behind that word 'tramp'.

'The views really are superb, aren't they,' she remarked pleasantly. But she knew that imp of mischief was stirring. 'Roseacres looks truly magnificent from far off,' she said. And could not, as she glanced around and saw that all eyes were on her, resist that imp as she added, 'Even from far off it looks colossal—it must be worth a fortune!'

It was interesting, she discovered, to watch the ice form in Matt's eyes as he caught her unveiled suggestion that in the absence of her grandfather having any real wealth, when the time came for the house and grounds to be sold on his demise, even taking into account that Matt, through his father's share of the house, would take half the proceeds, there would still be a tidy sum over to be shared between her and her cousins.

A stony silence had followed her remark. Though if Matt was withholding from saying something vitriolic—and it suddenly dawned on her that apart from that first meeting, he had been fairly polite to her in the company of others—then he need not have bothered. She thanked him for nothing.

'What a pity I shall be leaving in the morning,' she followed up, thinking perhaps she had the splendid meal to thank that she felt like taking the rise out of all of them once more.

'You're going back home tomorrow?' asked Josephine with the first sign of a pleasant look in her direction.

Such eagerness to see her gone from a cousin she had been prepared to like, momentarily flattened her. But it wasn't showing, as with matching pleasantness, she replied:

'I'd like to leave as early as possible.'

'There's a train at eight,' said the transparent Josephine. 'I'll run you to the station if you like.'

'I've never known you surface before nine,' put in Alain Todd grumpily, throwing his dinner napkin on to his dessert plate in irritation.

'I'm sure Josephine will make an exception in my case, won't you, cousin?' said Alandra, unable to avoid having acid in her tones as pride hurtled in that Josephine wouldn't have gone to bed if it meant she could assist her on her way any the quicker.

But, and it was with great surprise, Alandra found herself regretting her acid. For quite clearly, as her cousin went scarlet, she saw that Josephine, as empty-headed as she came across, was far more sensitive than she had imagined!

The impulse to apologise, even though if she couldn't take it Josephine should never have started it in the first place, was instantly squashed by the memory of the way her cousin had looked down her nose at her, and at her dress yesterday. She had more than a few acid remarks coming to her in her opinion, not least that she, like her brother, unaware that the transfer of Carstairs and Todd to Carstairs only on Friday had been a paper transfer only, thought like Matt, that she was only there for what she could get.

As she had done that morning at breakfast, suddenly Alandra left her chair. She had had enough of the lot of them, and couldn't wait to be on that train tomorrow.

'I'm going to bed,' she announced to no one in particular. And not expecting a reply, though as she had done last night, she heard a couple of chairs scrape back, she left the room.

They had been ready to move anyway, she mused, as not quite at the top of the stairs she heard the sound of voices and movement in the hall as they too left the dining room.

What they were saying she couldn't hear, but she wasn't interested anyway. Though Robert was getting it in the neck she plainly discovered by the sound of it. For suddenly she heard her grandfather bellow as on Saturday night she had heard him bellow, 'And for lord's sake, do something about your hair!'

Her ears were still ringing, making her wonder how Robert's ears were, since he was so much nearer to her grandfather than she was, when she let herself into her room with the thought, what a family!

Half an hour later, washed and changed into her cotton nightdress, she was in the middle of packing her dress into her case, thinking she would wear her jeans for the journey home in the morning, when to her surprise, not to say astonishment, the door of her room opened and the icy-eyed man she had last seen in the dining room was walking through it.

Alandra stood and gaped at him for all of five seconds, and it was the way Matt Carstairs was taking in the full shape of her breasts and where her nightdress clung to the outline of her hips, that had her shaking herself out of her stupefaction and quickly shrugging into her robe.

'If you'd timed it five minutes earlier,' she said tartly, 'you'd have caught me without a stitch on.' And still waspish, 'Try bruising your knuckles on the woodwork before you come in next time.'

'You're packing?' he queried, his tone sceptical, his eyes on the case on her bed.

'Brilliant,' she sneered. And in case he hadn't yet got the picture. 'I'd want paying to stay in this mausoleum.' Though before she could snap out the 'What do you want?' he was diverting her by reminding:

'You were nearly always broke, you said.' And while for a moment she looked at him wondering what was coming next, he asked, 'Are you still hard pressed?'

She shrugged, by his standards she was probably more than stony-broke. 'That's a crime?' she answered.

'You also said that you haven't a job at the moment.'

She still wasn't any nearer to getting on to his wavelength, but since he wasn't going to believe her anyway, she saw no reason not to tell him truthfully:

'Would you believe I gave up my job to look after my sick mother?'

He didn't believe it, which was all right by her. Though, when unexpectedly those unheralded tears pricked her again at the memory that she no longer had a mother in the flat in London, Matt Carstairs did get to the point of why he had, without so much as knocking, come into her room to repeat what she had told him in relation to her having no money and no job, and tears were shocked away, and it was her turn to look at him in disbelief.

'Would you mind,' she said faintly, still not believing it, 'repeating that?'

'I reminded you,' he complied, though his look told her she had heard him right the first time, 'that you have just said you would want paying to stay here.' And again, so Alandra could not possibly doubt her hearing a second time, he repeated, 'I'll do just that—I'll pay you to stay.'

CHAPTER FOUR

'YOU'LL—pay me . . .!'

Alandra still didn't believe she had heard what she had just heard. For a start, Matt Carstairs had never believed she had ever intended leaving anyhow. Although, with her case neatly packed including the paperback she had brought with her plus other incidentals, perhaps he was getting the general idea.

'Pull the other one,' she said getting ruffled, as suspicious about him as he was about her.

'I'm serious,' he told her impatiently.

He certainly did look serious, she had to admit. And that had her intrigued. Even with having to spend two nights under the roof of Roseacres being more than enough, she had to own to being not a little curious to know why—if indeed he was as serious as he looked and was not stringing her along for some devious reason of his own—he should make such a startling offer!

In her opinion, she considered it was time that she did a little stringing along of her own. 'You're willing to pay me to stay?' she asked quietly, her ruffled feelings covered by a ingenuous smile.

Her wide-eyed stare was discounted as she noted that his mouth, which on close inspection wasn't far from having a sensuous look to it, was firming into a tight line as he saw through the affected innocence of her smile.

'I've just said I would,' he told her briskly.

Alandra wasn't in a mind to let herself flare up at the shortness of his tone, though her eyes did spark briefly before she had herself under control.

'Take a seat,' she drawled, pointing to the beige-

coloured bedroom chair, and going to sit on the bed.
'This sounds more than interesting.'

Oh, wasn't he the one for tight-lipped looks? she
thought, as ignoring her offer he strode to the window,
his back to her, the drumming of his fingers on the sill
his way, she gathered, of counting to ten.

She had reached ten herself in her silent accompani-
ment, when the drumming stopped, and sharply Matt
Carstairs turned to look at her. His eyes flicked briefly
to her newly brushed pale gold hair, then went to her
eyes, then to her mouth, before, as though against his
will, he bit out, not meaning to astound her she felt
sure, though astounding her nevertheless:

'Your coming here has—cheered your grandfather
tremendously.'

'Cheered him!' she exclaimed incredulously, wondering what the dickens her sour-faced grandparent had
been like before. 'Are you meaning the same spleenish
man I'm thinking of?'

'The same,' he said crisply. 'You don't know him as I
do . . .'

'Nor do I want to,' she snapped, forgetful for a
moment of her intention to string him along.

'So you're admitting you only came here because of
what you read in the paper on Friday?'

God, was he quick with his assumptions! 'I'm
admitting nothing,' she flared, and had her work cut
out as she strove for calm. With difficulty she
swallowed her ire—oh, wouldn't she like to get back at
him! 'You were saying,' she said sweetly, 'that my being
here had cheered that delightful old man up. Am I to
assume you are offering to pay me to stay and keep him
at such effervescent cheerfulness?'

She gathered from the way Matt's hands went
thrusting into his trousers pockets as though clenched,
that he was hanging on grimly to keep his temper with
her.

'I've watched him since you've been here,' he said,

apparently having caught hold of the control he was after. 'I've seen the way he admires your spirit.'

'You *have* been observant,' she murmured, having personally missed any such expression about her grandfather.

'There isn't much I miss,' he replied rigidly, that double entendre there again telling her, if she didn't already know, that her grandfather had not been the only one he had been watching. 'I've seen him watching your reactions, the way he's noted your refusing to be put down by any of us.'

'You include yourself in line with him, in line with my snobby cousins?' she was in there, quick to ask.

'I have no time for snobbery,' he told her coldly, and little time for her either, she gathered. But she listened without interrupting when, observing that she wasn't going to come back with any pert answer, he went on, 'It has been of concern to me for some time now that Alain doesn't have the same—zest for life he once had.'

That she too should feel a prick of concern at his intimation that her grandfather might be ailing, irritated her. Let it be Matt Carstairs' concern, it was nothing to do with her, she thought, turning her back on it.

'He's getting older,' she said, making her voice sound heartless.

'He's sixty-nine,' Matt retorted. Then with a fresh effort to check his temper, more evenly he went on, 'To my mind his condition cannot be put down to just a normal ageing process.' And he unbent sufficiently to tell her, 'He used to roar about the place like a sergeant-major.' Having heard his roar a couple of times, Alandra thought in that case he couldn't have changed much. That was until Matt added, 'But it is only since your arrival that I've recently heard him bellow.'

And, she thought, discovered that you had missed it, and rather liked to hear the old devil roar. 'So you want me to stick around to keep the old fox barking?' she asked. But found that she had unbent a little too, when she added, 'You're fond of him.'

But again he was bouncing her own phrase back at her. 'That's a crime? I've known him all my life—he was like a father to me when my own father died.'

Alandra found herself wondering how old Matt had been when his father had died. And remembering her own vulnerability at that time, wondered, had he been at a vulnerable age too when he had lost his father?

Impetuosity, which she had to admit she wasn't short on, almost had her asking him, almost had her sympathising with him. But that was before common sense stirred and told her she was in danger of going soft on him. And he, she was fully aware, was a man it just wouldn't do to let see a chink in one's armour.

'That almost makes us related, doesn't it?' she said brightly. And on top now of that softer side that could be her undoing, 'I say, Matt,' she questioned, 'does that make us kissing cousins?'

Oh dear, she thought, as his brows came down and black clouds formed, Alandra Todd was the last person Matt Carstairs had it in mind to kiss.

'If you're thinking to "make up" to me,' he said, reminding her of her words at breakfast, 'then don't. I cut my teeth on your sort a long time ago.'

'Shame,' she retorted, bringing her mind back from wanting to wonder who she was, this woman—or was it women—who had soured him so she should get the sticky end. And striving to be serious, keeping her face straight, she asked, 'This paid employment, how long will the job last?'

'Let's say—three months,' he replied without so much as blinking.

'Three months!'

The exclamation had left her without thought, the idea of three months at Roseacres horrifying her. She would far rather serve a prison sentence, she thought.

But she was quickly collecting herself, giving him the impression she was thinking about it after all, when she still had every intention of being on that eight o'clock train in the morning.

'It will cost you,' she said more slowly.

'I've said I'll pay,' he reminded her shortly. 'If you agree to stay for three months, then at the end of that time I'll give you my cheque for a thousand pounds.'

He *was* as serious as he had said, she saw. He must be since they were getting down to the nitty-gritty of how much he was going to be out of pocket afterwards! And a thousand pounds, with board and lodgings thrown in—though she would still have to pay rent on her flat—wasn't bad, she had to admit. But the fact that he thought he could offer her money to stay in the same house with that irascible old devil, and that she would *accept*, made her blood boil, though she managed to hide it as she scorned:

'A thousand pounds! Is that all?' And jibing, 'It's no wonder you're a millionaire if you pay your lackeys such paltry wages.'

'My cheque to you will be a personal one, not one from Company funds,' he told her malevolently. 'And my lackeys, as you call them, are paid above the rate.' She could see he was near to boiling-point, too. But she had to give him full marks that he controlled his temper and left it simmering, to say, 'It won't be that hard a job, surely?'

'Have you seen him? Heard him?' she asked, when he knew her grandfather better than she would ever know him.

Matt didn't answer. But having given it to her straight, he was standing there, the lid only just down on his anger with her, she saw, and was waiting, expecting a straight answer from her.

She gave it to him, straight. 'You ask too much,' she told him. 'I couldn't do it.'

'Why?' He looked to be going nowhere in a hurry as

he challenged her for a reply, while all she wanted to do was to get into bed and go to sleep and forget about the whole insufferable lot of them. Then his look became thoughtful, and he went on to ask, 'Are you afraid your cousins will make things uncomfortable for you? If so I can . . .'

'My cousins,' Alandra jumped in heatedly, her pride out in front like a banner, 'can't touch me. They may have had everything that money can buy. They may have taken it upon themselves to look down their snobby noses at the poor relation. And they may be ashamed of me. But I'll tell you this for nothing, Matt Carstairs,' she said, green sparks shooting from her eyes, 'they are nowhere as near ashamed of me as I am of them!'

Having come to a furious end, she was regretting having let go so that only the truth had come spilling from her lips. But if her anger had gone out of control, she soon saw that Matt's anger, which earlier he had looked to be having a hard time in controlling, was nowhere about. And when for long moments he surveyed her, his expression as bland as it had been that morning, she realised she had never seen him so mild, before finally, he quietly dropped out:

'Then why not stay and show them what you're made of?'

In the face of his mild manner, her anger could not be sustained. Which was just as well, she thought, for all hell could have broken loose if he had come in to furiously defend the two people who, as with her grandfather, he knew far better than she did.

'To show them that I'm every bit as good as they are, you mean?' she questioned, sorely tempted to stay and take up the challenge.

'We were all born equal.'

'Some more equal than others,' she couldn't resist. And saw then, as he flicked a glance at his watch, that he was deciding he had spent sufficient of his time in putting the case to her.

And she wasn't at all surprised then, when with that touch of arrogance she was beginning to associate with him, he said, 'Well,' as if now was the time she could give him his answer, when as far as she was concerned, he had already received it in that 'You ask too much,' she had given him.

Well, two could play the arrogant game. Her chin tilted a little higher as she went to her bedroom door and held it wide. 'I'll think about it, and let you have my final answer in the morning,' she told him coolly as he started to move towards her.

He left without saying another word, but the glint in his eyes told her he wouldn't be averse to wringing her neck, and Alandra could tell that he was not well pleased at her determination to make him wait.

'And don't hold your breath,' she muttered as she closed the door after him. She didn't care tuppence whether he heard her or not.

But on climbing into bed, Alandra was to discover that, suddenly, she was far from sleepy. And it was through an age-long night where sleep seemed to come in half-hour snatches, knowing nothing would induce her to spend so much as one more night at Roseacres, that she just could not get out of her mind Matt Carstairs' strange offer.

She accepted that he must be fond of her grandfather that he had put aside his personal enmity with her to ask her to stay so she should cheer him up. But if what she had seen of her poker-faced relative was said to be more cheerful, then she was hopeful of being far away when his mood changed and his said cheerful disposition faded.

Awaking again from another half an hour or so of snatched sleep, Alandra felt wide awake. And although it was quite early, she decided that sprung mattress or no, she had had it with bed.

Moving quietly she washed and dressed, and fed up with thoughts of Matt's proposition that still dogged her, for all she thought it had been done to death in her wakeful night hours, she left her room and went silently downstairs.

. With no clear idea in mind of where she was going, she went along the hall and opened the door of the breakfast room, noting absently that the table was laid, probably done so last night by Mrs Pinder, she thought, as she wandered over to the French doors. The rose garden outside looked peaceful and beckoned, so that soon she had the bolts drawn back.

A minute later she was standing beneath an arch of deliciously scented pink roses, musing that here in such beautiful tranquillity, her mind might find peace from those thoughts that still chased around in her head. But it was not to be.

She had during the night, perhaps more asleep than awake, puzzled why Matt should invite her to stay on when he was so positive she was after her grandfather's money. But, there in the rose garden, the answer suddenly came to her without her even having to think about it.

Having informed her that her grandfather was not wealthy—though how that had come about since the firm according to her father had been flourishing when he had left home—Matt had seen she had nothing to gain but the thousand ponds he would give her if she stayed. And the fact that she might have designs on a share of the house and the land it stood on when her grandfather went to the happy hunting-ground, had not bothered him either; because sixty-nine he might be, but from what she had seen of him, her grandfather looked tough enough to snarl his way through another sixty-nine years. That in itself made it a long time before she would benefit from any scheming.

For the pure hell of it, she thought, bending her head to the scent of the roses, she would love to have stayed. For since Matt Carstairs dwelt at Roseacres too, she could see herself having a lovely time getting back at not only her high and mighty cousins, but *him* in particular.

A pity, she sighed, and then at long last had something else to turn her thoughts to. The sound in the stillness of the morning of the French doors opening, had her attention jerking to see her grandfather in casual trousers, a shirt, and a camel cardigan that had seen better days, stepping outside into the morning air.

She stayed where she was. She knew he had seen her, but if like yesterday morning all he was going to do was grunt in greeting, then as far as she was concerned, he could get on with it.

But to her surprise, when she wouldn't have put it past him to ignore her and go to inspect his rose beds elsewhere, he came slowly over to her.

'Good morning,' was forced from her lips when she had been meaning to make him speak first. And realising she was in danger of getting just like the rest of them, she forced a cheerfulness into her tones, and said, 'You're up bright and early.'

'I always am.'

'We do have something in common after all, then,' she said, and could have bitten her tongue. She didn't want to be like him, or any of them.

'Is that so surprising?'

Perhaps it wasn't, but she didn't want to go into that. 'Matt tells me you're sixty-nine,' she said, changing the subject. 'Have you retired from work?'

'I still occasionally go into the office,' he said, causing a strain of memory to stir in her.

'That'd be the office in Ferny Druffield?' she asked, knowledge with her somehow that that was where the firm had started out.

'Lord, we haven't had an office in Ferny Druffield this past ten years,' he replied. 'Though we have them most everywhere else.' He pulled a rose forward, seemed satisfied with its bouquet, and let it go, offering,

'The major plant is in Bedewick, ten miles away.' And, as an afterthought, 'The main offices are there too.' And acidly, 'Didn't you know?'

'If you're referring to the fact that the address of the firm was probably mentioned in the papers last Friday,' she said stiffly, her back coming up, 'then I'll tell you the same as I told Matt Carstairs—I didn't see a newspaper last Friday.'

'I wasn't meaning that,' he said, giving her a sharp look. 'I wondered if your father had bothered to keep track of what we were doing, that's all.'

'Did you keep track of what he was doing?' she questioned coolly, sensing censure she wasn't going to stand for in his tone.

He had no answer, and a grim silence followed so that she was in half a mind to go indoors. What kept her by her grandfather's side she had no idea, because he was doing nothing to break the disgruntled silence that had fallen.

And then, abruptly, her face solemn, taken unaware herself by the question that left her, she found herself asking, 'Why didn't you try to get in touch with my father after he left?'

'Why should I?' he replied, equally abrupt. 'He'd gone off with a penniless orphan, no chance there of the Todd name being carried on.' Alandra opened her mouth, but before she could say a word, he was taking the steam out of her, by saying, 'With not a word to your grandmother.'

She guessed her grandmother had been much loved by him, perhaps that was part of the reason he was such a crabby old misery. She had no idea when her grandmother had died, and, admitting a sensitivity she didn't want to have where her grandfather was concerned, she did not think that this was the moment to ask him. Instead, though still on the subject of love, she found herself asking:

'Didn't you love my father?'

Her question had him turning to look at her, his lined face as solemn as her smooth one. 'Love,' he said, 'is a two-sided angle, Alandra.' And while she was noting that he had called her by her given name for the first time since he had spoken it in exclamation, he was continuing, 'Edward could have contacted me too in all those years, you know—if he had loved me.'

He turned from her then, his hands going deliberately to toy with the rambling roses. And Alandra, in a sudden moment of insight, knew that there was emotion in her grandfather. Emotion he had turned from her to hide.

And quite without warning, there was emotion in her too. And there was not an ounce of the sauce in her to which she had treated him yesterday morning, as a softness came to her and she told him quietly, seriously:

'I think he must have loved you, Grandfather.' He made no sign that he had heard her, but kept his back to her. That was until, not wanting to say anything else, but seeming to have someone else in charge of her, she was unable to prevent herself from saying, 'I rather think I must have been named after you—I—don't think my father would have done that if he had no regard for you—do you?'

At that her grandfather did turn. And Alandra did see, for all he was trying to cover it, that there was emotion in him. His stern look had left him, and though there was no smile to be seen, his expression seemed softer, and, if she wasn't mistaken, there was a misty look to his eyes.

But he had nothing to say, and suddenly, a suspicion in her that he was too choked for words, that unexpected sensitivity in her where he was concerned had her searching for something to say to try and get him over the moment.

'Er—Matt has asked me to stay awhile,' she told him, when that had been going to be her secret. And damning her slippery tongue, she asked, 'What do you say about that?'

What she had expected him to say, she wasn't at all sure. But, as he took a moment to clear his throat before answering, what he did say was sufficient to have her staring at him in some surprise.

'It's his house,' he said, the intimation being that Matt could invite to stay anyone whom he pleased.

'His house!' she couldn't hide her surprise. 'But—but I thought you and Matt's father bought it between you way back when your wives were fed up with never seeing you?'

'That's how it was,' he agreed. Then he was thoughtful for some seconds before seeming to decide that since she was the only blood relative not in the know, there wasn't any reason why she shouldn't be brought up to date.

'Matt's father was killed in a traffic accident when Matt was fifteen,' he told her, his eyes glazing over as he remembered. 'That left me, with your father's help, in charge of the firm until Matt's education was finished.'

'But my father didn't like engineering?' she put in, and saw him frown, before he agreed:

'No, he didn't. He had no interest in the business at all—we almost came to blows about it many times. Anyway,' he said, passing quickly over what looked to be a painful memory, 'your father cleared out, and during the next few years Eunice's husband got into money trouble.' He didn't say what the trouble had been, but she guessed that her grandfather had bailed him out. 'Then your grandmother died,' he hesitated, then confessed, 'and things started to go badly at the plant.'

A picture was emerging for her, but trying to get it clearer, she asked, 'Matt was at university by this time?'

He nodded. 'I didn't have the heart to tell him how bad things were.' He cleared his throat, 'But by the time he was ready to start work, the firm was on its last legs.'

'Oh dear,' she said, visualising how dreadful he must have felt not to have been able to keep it from Matt any longer that the firm of which he owned half was going under. 'Was he very upset?'

'Matt, I then discovered, though I knew him as well as I thought I knew Edward by that time,' said her grandfather, 'is made of more practical stuff than to sit down and mope. When he sees there is a job to be done, he's the sort who rolls up his sleeves and gets in there and does it.'

Alandra could believe that, and wondered briefly if she came under the heading of a job to be done. Matt had seen, or thought he had seen, that her being there cheered her grandfather up. And though it must rankle that out of the affection he had for the man who in his adolescence had been like a father to him, he saw it as his duty to ask her to stay. Disliking her as much as she disliked him, he had rolled up his sleeves and asked her, not baulking at the task either for all he knew he was on a loser to start with. Perhaps that was why he had dangled that thousand-pound carrot.

'But what happened that the firm of Carstairs and Todd didn't go under?' she asked, coming back to the conversation that had been started with her revealing that Matt had asked her to stay awhile. 'I mean, if you had lost heart and Matt had come home fresh from university, he couldn't have got the firm back on its feet by himself, could he?' In her view, from what her grandfather had said, it would have taken a miracle to have done that and have got the firm where it was today.

'That he did,' he replied, his voice full of respect for the man she felt no admiration for. 'I helped out, of course, but I never did regain that enthusiasm I had when Matt's father and I first started out. That boy laboured night and day,' he said, admiration still there in his voice. 'He really stuck his neck out getting massive bank loans, and then he set about settling with my creditors, and, slowly at first, he pulled that burden up from the bottom of the hill from where I had let it slide.'

It sounded as though the whole of the Todd family had a lot to thank Matt for—though not her branch of the family of course. From the sound of it, her grandfather had been deeply in debt. But she wasn't interested in joining the Matt Carstairs fan club, so she went on to question:

'I understand about the firm going through a catastrophic time, but why sell the house?'

'Either Matt or the bank would have had my half share in it anyway,' he replied. 'My half was mortgaged. Matt used money he had inherited from his mother's side of the family to redeem it, and I was never more relieved that he did.'

Her grandfather had been very forthcoming, she thought, and realised then that it was a compliment to her that he had so unexpectedly done so. And, she thought, it had done him good to talk. He was certainly looking less emotional now than he had done.

'So not only does he own the house, but from what he tells me, Matt owns the firm too now.'

'Matt seems to tell you rather a lot!' was his shrewd statement. Which took her aback for a moment.

'Either you've got it or you haven't,' she said impishly. And realising she was on the verge of teasing him, which had from the outset never been her set course, she coughed, and said seriously, 'What about Robert?'

She had no love for her cousin, but it seemed to her then, that in selling out the firm, even if her grandfather had been hard pressed for a bit of capital, then any expectations that wild-haired young man had for his future didn't look to be worth having.

'Like your father, Robert isn't interested in engineering or the business,' he said. 'Though Matt has found him a place at the plant where he fools around for five days out of every seven.'

And suddenly, whether it was the memory of his son turning his back on what could have been his, or the thought of Robert being like-minded, Alain Todd was back to being the same grumpy old man Alandra had been sure, right up to this very morning, that he permanently was.

But if a change had come over him that he had opened up to her in the first place, she was to find that when as near as last night she very definitely would have left him alone to get on with it, all at once—or perhaps it had been steadily growing—a change had happened in her, too. He was sixty-nine after all, for heaven's sake, and even if he hadn't come right out and said so, suddenly she just knew he had loved her father; and that had to be all right by her. And it was just as suddenly that she found that she did want to tease him, and that she did want to try and get him out of his grumpy mood.

'I say, Grandfather,' she said, and knew that both her parents would have smiled if they could hear her, 'are you going to hold it against me that I'm a penniless orphan, too?'

For a moment when his cussed face remained stern, not so much as a movement on his crotchety mouth, Alandra wondered if she had gone too far. Blow you then, she thought. But then, magically, unbelievably, suddenly his mouth tweaked at the corners. And even if he did turn away to pluck one of the roses, just as if ashamed of anyone seeing his rare smile, a smile was what it was.

'Here,' he said, thrusting a rose that was just coming out of bud at her. And while she took it from him, realisation with her that he had picked it specially for her, his face fell into its usual solemn mask, as he grunted, 'You may be without parents, but you have a family—remember that.'

'Yes, Grandfather,' she said, and as he started to walk back to the French doors she fell into step with him. Quite suddenly, Alandra realised that she was feeling better this morning than she had any morning since her mother's death.

Not that that feeling was to last long. Matt Carstairs, dressed in a dark lounge suit which told her that nine o'clock would see him in Bedewick at work, was sitting at the breakfast table when her grandfather stepped back to allow her to go before him.

She guessed from the cold look he gave her that he had been watching her in the garden with her grandparent. And though it should have pleased him, had he seen like she had the self-ashamed smile, as she followed his eyes to the rose in her hand she saw that pleased was what he wasn't.

'Good morning, Matt,' she said, opting to provoke rather than ignore. And, finding the temptation too much, she couldn't resist the urge that came to hold her rose out in front and give it a twirl in his general direction.

By the look of him, her greeting going unreplied to, she rather gathered that he was regretting having asked her to stay. She took the same seat she had sat in yesterday morning, and while Matt and her grandfather exchanged a few comments, she fell to wondering why, since Matt didn't look to be overjoyed that to have been given a rose must mean that she was getting on quite well with the older man, if perhaps Matt, having not told her that he owned the house, thought she was still after the pickings that would result from the ultimate winding up of her grandfather's estate.

Mrs Pinder arrived just ahead of Josephine, the housekeeper going out to prepare the bacon and egg her grandfather had ordered rather than the porridge which Alandra gathered was his usual start to the day.

'Made it,' panted Josephine. 'I've just time for a cup of coffee, then I'll take you to catch the eight o'clock, Alandra.'

At once Alandra was aware of three pairs of eyes on her. Josephine's, she thought, were more friendly this morning than they had ever been. Well, she didn't need any prizes for guessing why, her dear cousin couldn't wait to speed her on her way.

'That really is most generous of you, Josephine,' she said, and unhurriedly she reached for a piece of toast.

Carefully, she then selected a pat of butter and placed it to the side of her plate, her eyes catching the icy blast of Matt's look. A further foray and a dollop of marmalade was beside the butter, her glance this time catching her grandfather looking at her, his expression chilling. Bleak House, she thought, and discovered her wayward tongue really did get her into the most difficult of situations.

'Now,' she said, since it appeared that everybody was waiting for her to say something more, 'having settled who is going to take me to catch the London train,' she glanced up, 'which one of you is going to be at the station to meet me when I come back tonight?'

Josephine was the first to break the silence that met her words. 'You're coming back!' she exclaimed, any friendliness in her soon departed.

'I wouldn't go at all,' she answered, aware that Mrs Pinder had come into the room and was on her way out again, 'but I really must pop to my flat and collect sufficient of my belongings to last me for an extended stay.'

'Make that two eggs, Mrs Pinder!' roared her grandfather in a voice that would shatter glass, obviously accepting that she was staying and having nothing to add to the conversation she and her cousin were having.

'You're going home for your clothes!'

Really, Alandra thought, feeling as cross with herself for having committed herself as she was with her cousin, Josephine who really was rather slow on the up-take.

'That's right,' she said, her eyes going to the icy look

of Matt Carstairs, 'I'm staying awhile.' Quite definitely, she thought, the owner of Carstairs and Todd, not to mention Roseacres, had gone off the suggestion he had made last night. 'I can think of a thousand reasons for staying,' she murmured.

And as the ice in Matt's eyes went glacial, she bit into her toast, happily aware that he was not appreciating at all that she was rubbing it in that he would be a thousand pounds out of pocket when she finally departed—or that she would need, as she had told him, to be paid to stay.

CHAPTER FIVE

IT was a fine Sunday afternoon and, having taken herself off for a walk, her mind on nothing in particular, Alandra realised that she was thinking that life at Roseacres was far more tolerable than she could have imagined a month ago.

She still wasn't sure how she had let her tongue be so unwary as to have her taking up the challenge of Matt Carstairs' invitation to stay. Though she rather thought that being goaded by each occupant in varying degrees might have had something to do with it.

Not that she had any intention of taking his thousand pounds when he offered it, but she was content to let him think that she would, just as she was content to let him think everything else he did about her. Pride would have her doing nothing to make him change his opinion of her. Her opinion of him that he was the most dislikeable man she had ever met had not altered, though quite when she had begun to change her mind about her cousins, about her grandfather even, she was still a little in the dark.

It had been easy to hate her grandfather when he had been an anonymous figure. Fairly easy, too, to dislike the cousins she had labelled stuck-up. But having lived with all of them for four weeks, having got to know more of each individual personality—save Matt Carstairs, and she reckoned she knew all she wanted to know about him to last her another two months—she had found that the labels she had hung around all three of them did not fit.

She had very soon seen that the reason why Robbie

had barely spoken to her that first weekend was because
he was shy. Even after having attended university, poor
Robbie was still painfully reserved.

Because he, like his sister, was always late down to
breakfast, she usually saw more of him at the evening
meal. But he was getting over his shyness with her, she
thought, and remembered last night at dinner when,
feeling his eyes on her, she had turned to give him a
friendly smile of encouragement, and her reward had
been to see him smile back.

Of course her smile had frozen when her glance had
caught Matt frowning at her. He had misread the
friendliness in her smile at Robbie, the disgruntled
flaring of his nostrils had told her that. He thought she
was setting her cap at her cousin, she had read that
plain enough.

She decided not to dwell on Matt Carstairs. She only
got cross when she thought about him anyway. Oh, he
was, on the surface, pleasant to her when anyone else
was around; good manners decreed that. And loathe
her though he might, he was doing his best to keep her
grandfather from knowing how much he detested her
and what he thought she was. But she knew that he was
still suspicious of her—look how he had misread her
motives with Robbie, for one!

Succeeding in ejecting him from her mind, Alandra's
thoughts latched on to her cousin Josephine. Jo was the
same age, twenty, that she was, she had discovered, but,
maybe because she had never had any responsibility in
her life, she appeared years younger. And though for all
she was a little feather-brained at times, after being at
first appalled at the very idea of her staying longer than
that one weekend, she had come round to being very
sweet to her.

Not that it had been that way to start with. Her
immaturity had had her being very disagreeable that
first week. But it was the second week when she had
come across her and Matt having a short sharp

exchange following his sarcastic enquiry about a letter in his hand that had just come for her.

'Some lover begging you to come back?' he had enquired, still holding on to the envelope she saw was in Hector's writing and probably contained an acknowledgment of the rent of her flat she had sent, having forgotten to give it to him when she had gone back to pack.

She had smiled then, and had infuriated Matt, as she had fully intended. Though she was unsure why crossing swords with him should always leave her feeling exhilarated, for he never had anything very pleasant to say in such encounters.

'I shouldn't be at all surprised,' she had said, her eyes wide. 'But he'll have to wait. I know which side my bread is buttered, don't I?'

'There was never any doubt in my mind about that,' he rapped. 'You . . .' he broke off as Josephine suddenly appeared from nowhere and stopped mid-transit.

'Are you two having a row?' she asked, her eyes going from Matt's angry expression, to Alandra, whose smile had suddenly gone into hiding.

'It's an occupational hazard in this house,' she snapped. And as without another word Matt pushed the letter into her hands and strode to his study, Alandra, spitting mad to have been deprived of standing up to him, went to march furiously up the stairs.

Only then did she discover that Josephine was right there beside her, saying hesitantly, 'Don't—you like Matt?'

And their near fight too recent for her to cover up, she had said shortly back, and with feeling, 'Like him! I hate the very sight of him!'

'Do you! I thought . . .'

And how Josephine's attitude had changed after that. Another week had passed and had seen her actually apologising for her earlier behaviour.

'Forget it,' Alandra advised. 'I expect you'd have acted the same with any woman under forty who looked like taking up residence.'

'Only if they were as beautiful as you,' Josephine replied with a grin, then went slightly pink as she realised that Alandra had seen what had been behind her affecting to look down on her and what she wore—her desire that she should leave with all speed. 'Is it so obvious?' she questioned.

'That you have a crush on Matt?' Alandra asked in reply, searching for tact.

'It's more than just a crush,' Josephine said, saving her from an answer. 'I love him. He was so good to me when Mummy and Daddy split up. He . . .' She broke off, suddenly alarmed. 'You won't tell him, will you?'

Alandra had a fair idea from the many times she had seen Matt fend off some of her cousin's more leading overtures that he had a fair idea already. But in the face of Jo's panic, she settled for:

'The only time Matt and I ever get talking is when we fight.'

Which had Jo's panic flying, and questions pouring from her on why it was she could not like Matt, when he was so . . .

Her cousin had used many adjectives to describe Matt Carstairs, Alandra reflected, as she turned about, thinking it time she went back to Roseacres. But none of the wonderful, marvellous, super names Jo had called him came anywhere near the overbearing, uncivil, growling-bear names she would personally have ascribed to him.

Matt was not at dinner that night, a fact Alandra greeted with pleasure, although she had to admit that the evening lacked sparkle. But that, she quickly concluded, was only because Jo was looking downcast that he wasn't there.

'Do you think he has a date?' her cousin questioned her grandfather.

'I shouldn't be at all surprised,' he replied grumpily. And sarcastically, 'It has been known.'

Nobody stayed down that night to watch TV or do anything else, except Alandra. After dinner Jo went straight to her room, and Alain Todd departed for his private sitting room to smoke his pipe. And although Robbie did sit with her for a while, after a half-hour where Alandra did her best to talk him over his shyness, conversation died, and he too went to his room.

Television on Sundays is boring, Alandra thought. At ten she went to bed, and she was as disgruntled as Jo had been when it dawned on her that with just one member of the family absent, and he wasn't really family for all they all lived in his house, everything seemed to go flat.

She was a long time getting to sleep that night. And to her consternation found she was wondering again and again what kind of woman it was who took Matt's fancy! It wasn't the first time he had skipped dinner to go out either, she mused, the possibility of his going steady coming to her.

She didn't like the thought, and reasoned that it was because Jo would be terribly upset if he came home one evening and told them that he was engaged.

In her attempt to get her mind away from Matt Carstairs, she channelled her thoughts to Robbie. Her efforts to get him over his shyness barrier had seen her asking him about his work at the plant. His reply had her knowing that her grandfather had been right to sell his half of it. Because it had very soon become obvious, that although Robbie might work there, it was only because he did not have the strength of character to tell the old man it was not what he wanted to do. Obvious, too, was the fact that once her grandfather was no longer there, her cousin would leave the firm of Carstairs and Todd, though what profession he would take up, it didn't appear that Robbie knew any more than she did.

After a fitful night, she was up early as usual the next morning, her waking thought to wonder if Matt had come home last night. How odd, she thought! But on going downstairs, she was able to see that it wasn't so odd that she should think of him on waking, because having spent one of those wakeful nights she occasionally experienced, she had not heard him come home.

'Beat me to it,' said her grandfather, coming from the French doors to join her in the rose garden.

'Good morning, Grandfather,' she greeted him, this the first time she had ventured into the rose garden since that first Monday morning when she had seen a one and only glimpse that he could be emotionally affected.

'You've got a hole in your cardigan,' she pointed out as he dug his hand in his pocket for his secateurs then snipped a piece of dead wood from a standard rose.

'Do you darn?' he grunted in his crabby fashion.

'Doesn't everybody?' she replied sweetly.

'Mrs Pinder cobbles.'

'So I'll darn it for you,' she said, and found herself smiling, an unlooked-for affection for her grandfather suddenly catching her unawares. 'Did Matt come home last night?' she questioned, her voice suddenly gone almost as gruff as her grandfather's.

'Not you too?' he said, straightening and giving her a shrewd look.

'Not what, me too?' she questioned back.

'Have you gone and fallen for him like your soft-headed cousin?' he asked point blank.

'Fallen . . .! For Matt Carstairs!' she said aghast. And recovering quickly, asked, 'How old do you have to be before they register you as senile?' She hadn't meant to say that, but appalled at the very idea, she was acidly refuting anything so unthinkable.

But her grandfather did not take offence. And if this was an instance of him, as Matt had said, admiring her spirit, though she rather thought her grandfather would dub it as sauce, she saw his apology for a rare smile break. And the next moment he was bent over a rose bush and had snipped off two roses.

'Forgive my weak brain,' he said, and with a surprisingly courtly gesture, he handed the two roses to her. 'I was just sounding you out. I didn't think I was mistaken that you and Matt are oil and water to each other.'

There was, Alandra decided, definitely nothing wrong with her grandfather's brain. He had looked beneath the surface of the cool civility she and Matt treated each other to in company, and had shrewdly seen that never would they mix.

'His mother should have boxed his ears far more than she did when he was a child,' she muttered, seeing no point in denying that she was not very well disposed towards the head of Carstairs and Todd, and her grandfather wouldn't thank her for blatant dishonesty. 'Where is his mother, by the way?' she asked, 'Did she die, too?'

'No, though she was so cut up when Matt's father died, I thought at the time it would have been a blessing if she had. Then she discovered painting, and because she started being plagued by rheumatism, she moved to Spain to live.'

Her mother had had rheumatic fever several times as a child, and that word rheumatism was enough to have Alandra's attitude mellowing as she and her grandfather strolled in the direction of the French doors.

She was through the French doors, her grandfather pausing to have a snip at something else, when she became aware that if Matt had stayed out on the tiles all night, then he had been business-suited and had made it back for breakfast.

She saw his eyes go to the two roses in her hand, his hard eyes travelling back up to her face. And as she recalled she had received a similar hard look from him that morning she had come through those selfsame doors carrying a single rose, so any of the mellowing that had visited her, promptly disappeared.

'Good morning, Matt,' she said perkily. And going to her place at the table she laid the two roses down by her plate. She observed that he was still watching her, and the words were bubbling out, 'Who knows, I may have a whole bouquet of them when I leave.'

'So long as you make sure that is all you leave with,' he threw at her.

And Alandra, not thinking anything he could say would hurt, felt just that emotion because he could make such an uncalled-for remark, even if she had done nothing to dispel the impression he had that she was there on the make.

But she was made of sterner stuff than to want him to witness that his barb had unexpectedly caught her. And her pride was in full sail, the hostile look that came to her eyes telling him his remark had bounced off her.

'I'll try and remember to leave a forwarding address so you can come and collect the family silver,' she tossed at him as, gracefully, she took her seat.

'You have a flat, I think you said?' She reached for the coffee pot, deciding not to answer. 'You never said where,' he pressed.

'Nor am I likely to,' she muttered, as habit had her stretching to fill his coffee cup.

'My mistake,' he said coolly, and waited for a moment as he retrieved his cup. But sarcasm was on its way, she knew it. 'I rather thought you were suggesting that I came calling.'

The coffee pot went down with a thud. Green sparking eyes looked into dark eyes that were as hostile as hers. 'That *is* an idea,' she said, watching his eyes narrow as he read that a not very polite dart was on its way. 'I live in a first floor flat. The idea of throwing a bucket of water over you has tremendous appeal.'

Her victory was only temporary, Alandra knew, as

whatever Matt had been going to come back with was
bitten back as her grandfather came through the French
doors. Some time soon her comment was going to be
returned, with interest, she was aware of that.

'Coffee, Grandfather?' she enquired. And she neither
looked nor spoke to Matt again during the time before
he left to go to his work.

September had given way to a glorious October. 'It
can't go on like this,' said Jo, having opted to go to the
village with Alandra to buy some darning wool to
match her grandfather's cardigan. She had suggested
that they make the trip in her car, but Alandra
preferred to walk, and Jo, though groaning at the idea,
had given in, and prattled on, when she wasn't speaking
of Matt, about the County ball being held in Bedewick
next week. Jo had mentioned the ball—just about
everyone would be there—in Alandra's hearing before,
though it had been Matt she had been speaking to, as
she had asked him if he was going.

'Is Matt going to go?' Alandra asked, with a
defeated, if you can't beat 'em, join 'em, feeling. Jo
would bring up the subject of Matt going or not going
any minute now anyway.

'I don't think so,' she replied pensively. 'I did ask
him, but he didn't look too thrilled. And then
Grandfather came and interrupted and I never did get
an answer.' But nothing if not tenacious where Matt
was concerned, she smiled, and a moment later was
resolving, 'I'll ask him again tonight.'

But they were halfway through dinner that night
before the subject of the ball came up. And launching
into the matter, although she prattled on and on, it was
not to Matt to whom Jo addressed her remarks, but to
her grandfather. He didn't look to be too thrilled either,
Alandra thought, as her cousin went on ceaselessly
about the band that had been hired, and about who
would be there. But finally, when she did come to an

end, it was with the question of could she please have a new dress.

Alandra was miles away, her lips twitching at Jo's strategy of wearying her grandfather with incessant chatter about the dance before she got in there with her request for a new dress, when suddenly Alain Todd surprised her into turning her attention on to him, when not replying to her cousin, testily he turned to Alandra and growled:

'Are you going to this wretched ball, too?'

About to give him a categorical 'No', for no reason her glance flicked to the other end of the table. Why Matt was favouring her with a frowning look, she didn't know. Though strangely she did believe he had been sincere when that one time he had stated that he considered everyone to have been born equal, so that ruled out that he was thinking that she wasn't good enough to join in with the County set. So why was he frowning? Because that was about the only expression he ever favoured her with, came the answer.

And suddenly that incorrigible imp of mischief that had never known when to lie down was asserting itself in her again. Her eyes were wide and innocent as she looked back to where her grandfather was waiting—not very patiently she noted from his dour expression—for her reply to his question of was she going to the wretched ball, too.

'Like Jo,' she said, a tinge of sadness in her tone, 'I've got nothing to wear.'

Perversity in her nature had her wanting Matt to believe she was trying to get a ball gown out of her grandfather, too. Let him think she was on the cadge, she thought, having no intention of setting foot inside Bedewick Guildhall next Tuesday night. She hoped with all her heart that her grandfather would play up to her, even if within the week he would know that she hadn't taken a penny from him for a new dress.

'I have heard it said,' he remarked with familiar

churlishness, 'that one's children keep one poor.' He hadn't finished yet, but as expectantly Alandra waited, she was soon to wish that the categorical 'No' that had hovered on the end of her tongue had been uttered. 'But,' he added to his waiting audience, 'nobody ever told me to watch out for granddaughters.'

While Jo let out a little squeal of pleasure that her grandfather had just agreed to her having a new dress, Alandra contented herself with a self-satisfied smile. She would love to have taken a look at Matt, but she wasn't sure she wouldn't break out into a fit of giggles if he was still frowning at her.

And then, Robbie, who as was usual had said very little during the meal, moved uncomfortably on his seat beside her. A second later, Alandra's feeling of wanting to giggle rapidly departed. For, as though screwing up all his courage, Robbie was addressing her:

'B-before anyone else asks,' he was saying in a rush, 'can I take you to the ball, Alandra?'

'But . . .' She broke off, what she could see of his ears were bright red, the "I'm not going" she had been going to utter sticking in her throat. The fact that she didn't know anyone else who was likely to ask her to the ball not of importance as that sensitivity in her picked up that Robbie was going to feel terrible if in front of everyone, she turned him down flat. Her smile had to be encouraging when it came, because already he was looking as though he wanted to hide under the table. 'I really can't think of anyone I would rather go with,' she said, and watched as an uncertain smile started to show in him until it grew to be a positive beam of delight.

He was still smiling, and had no objection to make, when Matt from the right of him pushed his chair back from the table and sent Jo into ecstasies by pronouncing:

'We'll all go together.'

Alandra's eyes shot to him, but having delivered his statement, nobody thinking to protest, Matt then strode from the room. Jo, with a hasty, 'Excuse me,' to her grandfather, chasing after him. And Robbie, still looking as if he couldn't believe his luck, went out too, muttering something about going to find his dress shirt so that Mrs Pinder could give it a swill through.

But Alandra, left alone with her grandfather, wasn't in any hurry to go anywhere. She was still sitting stunned, was still trying to sort out what had happened when, as little as ten minutes ago, she had very definitely not been going to go to the dance, suddenly, she was— and if she didn't want Robbie to lose some of his small supply of confidence, she just couldn't get out of it.

'You'd better get Josephine to take you into Bedewick,' said her grandfather when she had all but forgotten he was there. 'She'll take you to the shops where I have a charge account.'

That he was not smiling was to be expected. But she was learning to discern now when he was in a bad mood and when he was in a good mood. She rather thought his present mood fell into the latter category.

'I wasn't serious about having nothing to wear,' she told him stiffly. Though if she was honest, she knew she had nothing in her wardrobe that was remotely suitable for the occasion.

She heard her grandfather's teeth clamp down angrily, and guessed his mood was on the turn, as he irritably said:

'Going to go stubborn on me like your father?'

Alandra gave him an obstinate look. She didn't want him paying for her clothes. She would far rather not go, and that was a fact. But then she was remembering Robbie's face, his red ears. And suddenly, too, as she looked mutinously back into faded blue eyes, she was remembering the emotion that had been in them that particular Sunday. And it was then that she knew that if her mother had been hurt by this man and what he had written, then her grandfather had been hurt too— by her father. She wept less for her mother these days—

so had it been that, her emotions wildly off balance from finding that letter on top of her mother's death, these unsettling emotions were responsible for her coming here determined to hate? Here was her grandfather challenging her about going stubborn on him like her father, and, her memories of her father happy ones, she somehow knew that the obstinacy that seemed to run in the Todd side, would have been far better thrown out of the window. That, had both her father and his father not been so pig-headed, they could have made up their differences and her grandfather in particular would have been far happier.

'Well?' he prompted crustily, seeming to think he had given her enough time to decide if she was going to be stubborn about letting him pay for her dress.

'Blackmailer,' she said, giving in. But she saw from the twinkle that was all at once there in his eyes, that she had pleased him. 'Are you going to this "wretched ball", too?' she asked him sourly.

A definite smile lurking, he shook his head. 'Matt will look after you if you're nervous about being introduced as a member of this family,' he said, something she was not at all nervous about simply because she hadn't given the matter any thought. 'Though knowing you,' he conceded, 'you'll transmogrify the first one who dares to wonder why we have kept you hidden.'

'Must remember to take my broomstick,' she said dryly, but she had to laugh.

The following morning saw Alandra going with her cousin to scour the shops in Bedewick for the dresses they were to buy. Jo was quickly fixed up with a full-skirted flowery confection that was exactly her. And delighted with her purchase, her enthusiasm was endless to find something for Alandra.

But it was not until they came across a chiffon-covered red satin off-the-shoulder dress, its full skirt a dream, that Alandra felt the first stirrings of enthusiasm herself. And even while telling herself that she didn't want the dress, just as she didn't want to go to what was firmly fixed in her head now as 'the wretched ball', once she had seen herself in the red dress, her waist looking tinier than ever in the wide cummerbund, she had to own a flutter of excitement.

Though she was to frown momentarily when in her mind's eye she saw Matt, not Robbie her escort, waiting at the bottom of the stairs, his eyes fixed on her as she floated down them.

She blinked, and the picture had gone. How peculiar, she thought, banishing Matt Carstairs from her mind. Though it was no wonder he seemed to be always in her head these days—never had she met a more odious creature.

By the time the weekend had arrived, Alandra, getting ready to go down to dinner, had lost all enthusiasm and excitement when she thought of the forthcoming ball. And it had nothing to do with the second thoughts that had visited her about giving in and allowing her grandfather to pay for her dress. She had been able to push those second thoughts away on realising the pleasure it had given him that she had accepted his gift. He *did* seem more cheerful these days—she could only wish she felt the same.

But she was finding it not so easy to push away the root cause of what was bothering her—the reason why she had gone off all idea of going to the ball. It was Robbie—Robbie and his attitude that was bothering her.

For ever since she had accepted his invitation, he had begun paying her more marked attention than by just agreeing to go to the dance with him should encourage him to do. And since she didn't want to hurt his feelings for fear she should set his emergence from his shyness back, she was in a quandary to know what to do about it.

Had she not seen he appeared afraid of his grandfather, she might have had a word in his ear. But the situation needed a little finesse, and she couldn't see the old man handling it with anything that didn't resemble a bull at a gate.

Why she should think of Matt as the only man to handle the matter delicately, she couldn't imagine, because where she was concerned he didn't hesitate with his own brand of blunt tactics. And anyway, if the searing look she had received from him last night when red wine had gone slopping all over the table as Robbie in his haste to top up her glass had been all fingers and thumbs, was anything to go by, then she rather thought he was of the opinion, by the very fact she had accepted Robbie's invitation, that she was egging Robbie on.

Still disturbed and deciding that tonight she wasn't going to have any wine, she left her room and joined the others in the drawing room at a minute before eight.

'There you are, Alandra!' said Robbie, his shyness for the moment absent as he came over to her. 'I thought your watch must have stopped or something.'

Helplessly, because there was nothing else she could do, Alandra smiled at him, her glance catching the cold glint in Matt's eyes as over the top of Jo's head he looked furiously at her.

'My tummy always tells me what time it is,' she said lightly, Robbie hanging on every word. 'I'm starving,' she lied.

Throughout dinner she felt constrained to swallow, aware as she was that not only was Robbie looking at her a good deal of the time, but that Matt was observing the pair of them and was getting more and more tight-lipped.

To her mind the meal went on forever, but at last, nerves getting to her, a point came where she could be first to leave the room without anyone raising an eyebrow. Casually, too casually, she placed her napkin down beside her plate, but only for it to slip, Robbie there instantly to catch it and return it to the table.

'Thank you,' she murmured, and fibbed, 'If you'll excuse me, I have a few letters to write.'

She didn't hang about then, and though hearing other chairs being pushed back she kept her eyes on the door making for it with a dignified speed. A small sigh of relief left her at being free of Matt's dark looks and Robbie's spaniel-eyed expression. But any relief she felt was short-lived. For she had not gone more than a few yards when she heard someone else had left the dining room and was right there behind her.

Robbie! was her first thought. But she did not have time for a second, because a hard hand snaked out to encircle her wrist, and the next thing she knew was that she was being yanked by the arm without either word or courtesy. Suddenly she was closeted in Matt Carstairs' study with the door slammed firmly shut telling anyone interested to keep out. Then Matt was turning her to face him, and her spirit quailed—because his eyes were positively blazing!

CHAPTER SIX

ALANDRA stared stupefied into Matt Carstairs' furious eyes which were so flaming, pinpoints of yellow seemed to be flashing out at her from his irises. But that was all that she did have time to observe, because, without giving her a moment in which to regain her breath after being hauled so unceremoniously into the study, he was flaying into her hot and strong, flinging her wrist distastefully from him as he snarled:

'What the hell do you think you're doing?'

'What do I think *I'm* doing,' she shot straight back, her wrist sore from his man-handling, but a wrist that could drop off before her pride would have her letting him see her rub it. 'Caveman tactics may go down well with women of your usual acquaintance, but in London we're a little more civilised.'

'You're not in London now,' he rapped brusquely. 'You're in the country where we might appear a trifle less sophisticated . . .'

'You're saying you're not sophisticated, Matt!' she dared to jibe, not believing it for an instant. 'Surely not?'

'I'm not talking about me,' he threw at her cuttingly. 'And you know damn well I'm not.'

She hadn't known, but what he had said told her precisely who they were talking about. And it had crossed her mind to approach him to have a word with Robbie! Definitely not. She didn't need too much intelligence to know that Matt had seen, as she had, that Robbie had a bit of a crush on her—but, oh so very clearly, Matt didn't like it.

'So we're talking about Robbie?' she challenged, it not being in her nature to back down.

'Got it in one,' he said fiercely. And proceeded to make her furious by not seeing that Robbie's crush on her was none of her making, or that it was something she did not want, but dared to assume that she was leading him on. 'Lay off him,' he told her bluntly. 'He can't handle a girl like you and you know damn well he can't.'

About to flare up again, his belittling 'a girl like you' hit, and the heat in her was cooled to cold anger. It was as clear as day that being fond of her whole family, there was one member she had no regard for at all. Well *let* him damn well worry about Robbie, she thought, and was not then in a mind to make it any easier for him.

Her manner off-hand, but seething inwardly, casually she shrugged. 'What's a city girl to do?' she asked. 'You must see how deadly dull it is around here—and a girl has to keep her hand in.' Coyly she smiled, 'And you, if you remember, dear Matt, have told me point-blank that I'd be wasting my time pursuing you.'

If she was coldly angry, then she saw that his anger had turned to icy fury as her words reached him. 'You . . .' he bit out. But just when it looked as though he was going to grab hold of her, the phone on his desk started to shrill for attention.

'Saved by the bell,' she muttered mockingly.

But she was beginning to wonder if she had been been as Matt made no move to answer it. It was only when she saw the irritated way his hand went to the persistent instrument, no one else in the house apparently concerned enough to pick up the call on any of the various extensions, that she dared to move to the door, saying, 'What's it worth—to lay off Robbie?'

That she had misjudged her man had passed Alandra by in her lofty 'take that to think about' mood as she went to leave him to chew on it. For her hand never made it as far as the door handle before his hand had shot out and he had gripped her wrist again in a vicelike hold; the look in his eyes telling her that he hadn't finished with her yet by a long way, as he barked, 'Carstairs,' down the phone.

His eyes had gone from her briefly, but they came flashing back as keeping that tight grip on her, he barked again, 'Who's calling?'

Alandra was starting to feel sorry for whoever it was who was calling, while wishing she could free her wrist from Matt's burning hold—perhaps a kick on the shins might do it? Then as he suddenly thrust the instrument at her, she realised that the call was for her! Though since he must know the name of her caller, she noted he was keeping it to himself.

She took the phone from him, saying, 'Hello,' while doing her best to ignore that Matt Carstairs, ignorant pig, wasn't going anywhere if this was a personal call for her—though she hadn't any idea who it could be.

'Who the dickens was that?' questioned a male voice which she couldn't place, but which sounded familiar. 'Do you think I could sell him a policy against the mishap of sounding civil when he answers the phone?'

'Hector!' she exclaimed, pure pleasure only in her voice. Hector had been more like a friend to her than employer and landlord, and she was fond of both him and his wife.

'Thought my Hercule Poirot bit would amaze you,' Hector chuckled, going on to explain that when he had needed desperately to get in touch with her he had re-read the letter she had sent forwarding her rent. In her letter, he reminded her, she had said she was staying with her father's family for a while, so he had looked up Todd in the telephone directory and—hey presto!

Alandra thought it was lucky that the Roseacres number was listed separately under the names Carstairs and Todd, and wished the former would leave the study—for all he had more right there than she—because she wasn't finding it at all easy to ignore him.

'Your need to contact me was desperate?' she questioned, from the corner of her eyes noting that Matt was looking grimmer than ever.

'That perishing woman I took on to replace you has given notice,' said Hector sounding offended, getting to the point of his call. 'She isn't any good, anyway,' he said in self-defence. 'I was wondering if you felt like coming back?'

'I . . .' she began, then hesitated as Matt made an impatient movement signifying that he wasn't growing any sweeter tempered to be kept waiting in his belief that he was going to sort her out. 'The idea really appeals, Hector,' she told him, and unable to deny herself the pleasure of getting one in. 'But, unfortunately, I can't leave here for a while.' Her tone now confiding, 'Actually, I'm doing a temporary job at the moment.'

'You're working!'

'It's only temporary, as I said, and . . .' she took a quick glance at Matt, seeing with satisfaction that he wasn't missing a word—oh when, she wondered, noting his compressed lips, had she ever thought he had a generous mouth—'and although the job doesn't pay very much, there's a splendid chance I might receive a bonus at the end . . .' The 'of it' she had been about to say, never got said, for Matt Carstairs had had enough. And then several things happened at once.

He was tall and fit was Matt, and never had she known a man move more quickly. One moment she was sending him up for all she was worth, but the next the phone had gone from her grasp and had gone crashing back on its cradle as a furious hand wrenched it from her. And while she was trying not to admit that her stomach was somersaulting wildly in panic at the look on his face that said strangulation was just about to be performed, the door opened and Jo poked her head in, her cry of, 'I thought I heard the ph . . .' breaking off as she, too, witnessed that Matt looked just about to commit murder.

Then, while Matt's hands clenched by his sides and Alandra tried to compose herself and effected to make it look as though she walked from a death threat every day of the week, Jo was apologising, saying:

'Sorry, I didn't mean to interrupt if you two are having another row.'

'Feel free,' said Alandra after a struggle, making a bee-line for the open door. 'We'd just about finished, hadn't we, Matt?' And not giving him the chance to say anything, but thinking discretion was the better part of valour if he hadn't finished, she made her escape.

But she had been shaken by the violence she had witnessed in Matt, even if she was aware that it had been her impudence that had pushed him that little bit too far. And though she was sure that she wasn't a coward, it was further discretion telling her it would be wiser to keep out of his way for a day or two, that had her avoiding him.

Her grandfather had said they were like oil and water to each other, but she was of the opinion that they were more like some highly volatile substances that only needed a spark to set them both off. And since, by now aware of what lay where in connection with the house, the door to the apartment Matt had on the first floor exactly opposite hers, Alandra found herself pausing before she left her room and listening for any sound that would tell her that Matt was about.

By the time the night of the ball arrived she was on the way to forgetting that scene in the study, though what Hector had thought of the abrupt termination of his telephone call, she couldn't begin to think. And Matt, she thought, had put the scene behind him too, for although she was aware that his eyes were frequently on her, especially when Robbie was around, last night he had quite civilly offered her a sherry when she had joined them in the drawing room before dinner.

And he was quite civil too, she considered, when ready to go to the Guildhall, the four of them assembled in the hall, and he suggested it was time they were on their way.

Jo made straight for the front passenger seat, and with Robbie's assistance, Alandra stepped into the back. Come back all I said about Matt just missing being handsome, she thought, recalling again the strange sensation she had experienced when she had first seen him kitted out in his dress suit—he looked terrific! Robbie too, Alandra made herself think as the car sped towards Bedewick, Jo chattering ten to the dozen, the young man looked different tonight. Somebody had actually had a go at his hair!

At the Guildhall, she and Jo went to check in their cloaks and run combs through her hair, Alandra's cloak was by courtesy of a loan from her cousin.

'Wow, wait till they get a look at you!' said Jo as the two girls stood side by side looking into the tall and wide mirror in the cloakroom.

'Have you seen yourself?' Alandra laughed. Jo looked quite lovely, she thought, in her floral dress.

Jo grinned, but her eyes were on Alandra who in a self-conscious movement, unused to such finery, was fingering the pearls which, after a tussle with her grandfather in his sitting room, she was wearing.

'Are those Grandmother's?' Jo questioned, still smiling, obviously, Alandra thought, having seen the pearls before.

'Yes, do you mind?' she quickly asked. 'Grandfather insisted, and I . . .'

'Of course I don't mind,' said Jo holding up her wrist and showing off the most gorgeous bracelet. 'I'm wearing Grandmother's diamonds.'

Alandra experienced another moment of self-consciousness when she and Jo walked to where Matt and Robbie were waiting for them. This was the first time either of the men had seen them without their cloaks, and suddenly she was overwhelmingly aware of her naked shoulders and the amount of bosom she was showing—slight when looked at directly, but with Matt's height as he moved to the side of her, enough to have a faint touch of pink touching her cheeks as he looked down at her.

But when she flicked her eyes to look up at him, it was not her bosom that held his interest, she saw, but the pearls that adorned her throat. And even though for once she did not want to fight with him, that recalcitrant spirit in her that just had to get in first, had her eyes going wide as she addressed her quiet remark directly at him.

'A nice gift, aren't they?'

'Alain *gave* them to you?' he questioned, and suddenly she could have hit him.

She was grateful then that some people the family were acquainted with came up to them, and in the general introductions and ensuing exclamations that followed, Matt introducing her as Alain Todd's other granddaughter, her urge to thump him got swallowed up.

Had Robbie had his way, he would have had every dance with Alandra. But as one hour went by, and then two, he had his work cut out in getting more than three dances with her. For although she had not danced with Matt, who appeared to be a lamp all the moths flitted around—correction, butterflies fitted better, she thought—she had not been lacking for partners.

'It was a mistake to come on my first date with you where all the other men in Bedewick have gathered,' grumbled Robbie, the one or two trips she had seen him making to the bar going a long way to help him overcome his shyness.

Alandra managed to keep smiling, not too happy with his comment about this being their first date, and wondering how she could refuse a second without hurting his feelings.

Say Hello to Yesterday
Holly Weston had done it all alone.

She had raised her small son and worked her way up to features writer for a major newspaper. Still the bitterness of the the past seven years lingered.

She had been very young when she married Nick Falconer—but old enough to lose her heart completely when he left. Despite her success in her new life, her old one haunted her.

But it was over and done with—until an assignment in Greece brought her face to face with Nick, and all she was trying to forget....

Time of the Temptress
The game must be played his way!

Rebellion against a cushioned, controlled life had landed Eve Tarrant in Africa. Now only the tough mercenary Wade O'Mara stood between her and possible death in the wild, revolution-torn jungle.

But the real danger was Wade himself—he had made Eve aware of herself as a woman.

"I saved your neck, so you feel you owe me something," Wade said. "But you don't owe me a thing, Eve. Get away from me." She knew she could make him lose his head if she tried. But that wouldn't solve anything....

Your Romantic Adventure Starts Here.

Born Out of Love
It had to be coincidence!

Charlotte stared at the man through a mist of confusion. It was Logan. An older Logan, of course, but unmistakably the man who had ravaged her emotions and then abandoned her all those years ago.

She ought to feel angry. She ought to feel resentful and cheated. Instead, she was apprehensive—terrified at the complications he could create.

"We are not through, Charlotte," he told her flatly. "I sometimes think we haven't even begun."

Man's World
Kate was finished with love for good.

Kate's new boss, features editor Eliot Holman, might have devastating charms—but Kate couldn't care less, even if it was obvious that he was interested in her.

Everyone, including Eliot, thought Kate was grieving over the loss of her husband, Toby. She kept it a carefully guarded secret just how cruelly Toby had treated her and how terrified she was of trusting men again.

But Eliot refused to leave her alone, which only served to infuriate her. He was no different from any other man... or was he?

'I like your hair cut,' she said, turning the subject from what could be dangerous waters.

He smiled, pleased she had noticed. Though in her view since two thirds of his mop looked to have been thinned out, it would have been remarkable had she not noticed.

'Matt sent me along to his barber this afternoon with instructions not to come back until I looked nearer a skin-head,' he told her.

It was Robbie who took her into the buffet supper. But they were not to eat by themselves, even if he did say he would have preferred it that way.

'Aren't you going to introduce me to your cousin?' said one young man she had not yet danced with, but who had clearly got to hear of their blood relationship.

'If I must,' said Robbie, not very graciously, introducing the fair-haired Dudley Millar, and emitting a groan when another young man about the same age, whom Alandra did recall having danced with, came and stood with them. 'And I suppose you want an introduction too, Morgan?'

'We've met,' replied Nigel Morgan with a grin of some charm. 'Can I have the first dance after the interval, Alandra?'

'Alandra came with me,' stated Robbie, firmly staking his claim.

'Cousins don't count,' said Nigel, his blue eyes twinkling, 'Do they, Robbie's cousin?'

Alandra had to smile back. 'Where's Jo?' she asked, fending off having to answer. 'I haven't seen her in an age.'

'Last time I saw her she was with Jonathan Naseby,' replied Dudley. Which left her then wondering where Matt was, though that was one question she refrained from putting.

They had all but finished eating when she saw Matt enter the supper room. She watched him and saw his eyes flick round until they lighted on her and the three men she was with. And for a moment she thought he was going to come over, and she felt her heart take the most idiotic upswing. Most idiotic, she considered, since over two hours had passed and not once had he approached her for a dance, so therefore she wasn't a bit bothered about him either.

He did not come over to where she and Robbie were. And it was not long afterwards that, the supper interval over, she saw him smiling—something he never did with her—as he stood talking to a female of about thirty, who looked stunning in her slinky gold lamé dress, her hair as black as jet done up in a very becoming chignon.

Suddenly, having danced again with Nigel and once with Dudley, Alandra began to wish it was time to go home. She had seen Jo float by looking animated as she looked up at her partner. Robbie had again made an excursion to the bar. And Matt was making no move to get away from the dark-haired woman, so presumably, he was enjoying himself.

It had gone midnight and Alandra was dancing with a man more mature than Robbie and the other men she had danced with, when she wondered for how much longer it would go on. It seemed a bit pointed to ask, she thought, and might well give the impression that she was not having the whale of a time that she was trying to make out she was having.

'Do you live in Bedewick?' asked her partner, one person out of all those who had come up to her who didn't know who she was, apparently.

'I'm staying in Ferny Druffield with some relatives for a while,' she told him. And passing the spot where last she had seen Matt, she gave a surreptitious glance to see he must now be dancing, for there was no sign of Matt or his stunning companion.

'Ferny Druffield!' exclaimed her partner, 'I live not a stone's throw away from there. Perhaps I could call and take you . . .'

Before he could finish his invitation, or before she

had the chance to give him the evasive answer that was hovering, someone had come to interrupt. And with an ease that left her staring, Matt Carstairs had cut in with a not to be argued with:

'Have you forgotten you promised the next waltz to me?'

Still gasping at the smoothness of the way he had taken her from her partner's arms, Alandra found she was in Matt's arms and was being danced away in perfect time to the music.

He was a good dancer she had to admit, as she refused to get mad at him in case her unwary tongue led them into pitched battle right there in the middle of the dance floor. And although she had had, apart from this evening, very little practice, the fact that he was a good dancer made her feel that she wasn't too heavy on her feet either.

'Do you always cut in to tell lies about a promise to dance with someone you have only just remembered came in the same car with you?' she asked, when having circuited the floor once without Matt saying a word, she thought she had sufficient control to cope with whatever he answered.

'Do you think I am ever likely to forget you?' he replied suavely, his glance down taking in the creamy upper curve of her breasts.

'I'll make sure you don't,' she said sweetly. She hadn't missed his sarcasm.

Though oddly, instead of needing her control then to keep her from going into verbal battle, she discovered that his sarcasm had made tears prick her eyes, her control needed to get over what she considered had to be the oddest thing to date. Matt never had *that* effect on her, she thought. Always before she had been ready to jump in to meet him in battle. And always after a fight, she had come out, if on occasions licking her wounds a trifle, then at least not without a feeling of exhilaration from trying to notch up a few chalk marks of her own.

'What's the matter?'

His question surprised her, until she realised that Matt was too sharp not to notice that the comment she had made was a shade mild for her.

'What time does this function end?' she asked, past caring who knew that she wanted to leave.

'I expect it is a mite tame for you after the life you led in London,' he came back, as ready as ever to needle, she thought.

'I have to admit that it is—different,' she said, trying to buck up as the waltz came to an end, but her heart not really in it.

She went to walk away from him when the dancers started leaving the floor. And looked her surprise when Matt kept hold of her arm.

'We'll round the other two up,' he answered her questioning look, the hardness in his eyes telling her that far be it from him to force her to attend any hick-town ball if she felt that way about it.

'But Jo might be having a good time!' she felt honour bound to protest.

'And Robbie might be trying to drink the bar dry that you agreed to come with him, yet ditched him the moment you saw there was a wealth of male talent locally.'

'It would appear,' she said acidly, 'that I can't win either way. On the one hand you tell me to lay off Robbie, and when I do just that, you accuse me of forgetting my manners.'

'Don't worry about it, Alandra dear,' he mocked. 'We have a ten-mile drive home—plenty of time for you to tell Robbie you didn't really mean to dance with half of Bedewick.'

If she had been his mother, Alandra thought, Matt Carstairs would be nursing a couple of cauliflower ears by now. Especially when just as she spotted Jo, Matt obviously knowing where she was all along since they were heading in her direction, he remarked, still mocking:

'Though if you think you might have your work cut out handling that young man on the way back, you can always sit up front with me.'

'The man hasn't been born yet whom I can't handle,' she hissed at him.

But, as the car sped away from Bedewick and a flushed-faced Robbie, his shyness drowned in alcohol, went to take her in his arms, Alandra found she was fighting a silent battle to keep his hands off her for most of the journey. She was aware that a frowning full use was being made of the rear-view mirror, and by the time they decamped at Roseacres, she would sincerely have loved to knock two male heads together.

Alain Todd had gone to bed by the time the three of them walked into the hall, and the fourth one walked the best way he could.

'You'd better get to bed, Robbie,' Matt told him, as spotting Alandra had not yet moved to the stairs, Robbie staggered over to her.

'Come—to—bed wiv me,' he slurred to her when, it looking as though he was going to fall flat on his face, she quickly put a supportive arm around him.

'Bed—alone!' said Matt in a muted roar. And the last she saw of him was Matt marching him up the stairs.

'He didn't mean it,' said Jo, excusing her brother. 'He's sloshed. He'll die a thousand deaths tomorrow if he remembers any of it.'

'I know,' said Alandra sympathetically, starting to mount the stairs. She wasn't in a mood for conversation. She felt down, offended by Robbie's remark even if he was sloshed. All she wanted to do was to get to bed and to get to sleep. But Jo wasn't looking very happy either. And anxious that she shouldn't feel uncomfortable on account of her brother's drunken remark, she asked, 'Did you have a good time?'

'So-so,' said Jo, not looking any happier.

'But I thought you were thoroughly enjoying

yourself,' she said, recalling her cousin's animated look as she had danced by her.

'I think I must be schizo,' Jo replied. 'Half of me thought the evening terrific—the other half died when I saw *La* Hamilton was back in town.'

'Oh,' said Alandra, guessing that the dark-haired beauty must be *La* Hamilton, and very probably an old flame of Matt's.

'Oh, is right,' said Jo, and as she reached her door. 'Goodnight, Alandra.'

The house had been quiet for some time when wide awake, no longer looking forward to her bed, sleep miles away, Alandra knew a restlessness of spirit. She had taken off the pearls and had started to undo her dress, when not knowing what she wanted, or why she should feel so, she re-zipped her dress and feeling unsettled, stifled in a house where her cousin Robbie had taken a shine to her, and where Matt Carstairs viewed her only with loathing because of it, she sighed and knew she had to get outside.

She hadn't meant to hurt Robbie, but hurt he had been, she knew that. And she sighed again, as with too much on her mind she tiptoed down the stairs and passed through the breakfast room and out through the French doors—her mind too full to notice that she did not need to unbolt the doors.

Her feet went silently over the dewy grass until she reached a rose arbour. And there she stopped, her mind a mixture of sympathy and anger with Robbie. She had been right to treat him as a cousin at the dance, she knew she had, but in view of his getting tight she was belaboured by conscience that said she shouldn't have danced with all and sundry just to get her point across.

Though whatever she did wouldn't be right in Matt Carstairs' eyes, she thought. And she hated him afresh as she absently paced up and down. That was until she very nearly jumped out of her skin to hear in the silence of the night a quiet voice she had no trouble in recognising, as he enquired:

'Restless, Alandra?'

How long he had been standing there watching her, she had no idea. But as she spun round she was able to make out the shape and size of Matt and his white shirt front as he came out of the shadows.

The fact that her heart had begun to race alarmingly was all on account of the shock she had received. Whose heart wouldn't pound on believing they had the rose garden to themselves, only to discover in the darkness that they hadn't? And it was for that reason too, she knew, as he came to stand within a yard of her, that her throat dried and she could think of nothing to say.

'Restless because I cut in before Frank Millington could complete his arrangements for a romantic interlude?' he continued, enlightening her as to the name of the man she had been waltzing with, nothing wrong with his hearing that he had picked up what was being said.

'Romantic interlude?' she echoed, at last finding her voice, but an inability in her to find the fire with which she usually met any attack from Matt.

'From the way you were going at it tonight, you were obviously trying to make up for the nun-like existence you've been forced to adopt this past month,' he remarked, his tone changing, a sting in his words that even in shock, her temper wouldn't stay down for.

'Had I been interested in a romantic interlude as you call it,' she hissed, her tongue running away with her, 'Robbie would have done.'

'But Robbie was a little worse for wear, wasn't he?' he said, his voice short. And then coolly, he just about topped everything he had ever said to her, by jibing, 'Is that why you came looking for me?'

'Looking for you!' For a moment she was slow to get his meaning. 'I didn't even know . . .' she began, then as his meaning found its mark, fury broke in her that he could think such a thing. 'Why you conceited ...' Words failed her as she remembered the beautiful women who had fluttered around him that evening. 'Other women might fawn all over you, Matt Carstairs—but I'm not one of them,' she told him hotly.

'And you're not looking for a romantic alliance either, are you?' he scorned.

And then suddenly, while she was still spitting fire, just as though something in him had snapped, his thin patience run out, he had moved that one step forward, and he was taking hold of her. And his voice was grating in her ears as he hauled her up against him and didn't look like letting her go.

'We'll prove that, shall we.'

And before his intention had time to register, Alandra felt his mouth come down over hers, and she was then being soundly kissed by the one man she hated above all others.

Which made it stranger than ever, she thought, knowing herself bemused, that when for a few seconds she struggled madly in his arms, Matt, in full control as he held her firmly against him, should suddenly have the fire of temper going out of her, and a fire of a sort she was slow to recognise begin to kindle inside her.

'Stop it,' she protested, when his mouth left hers and she felt a whisper of warm kisses trail over her bare shoulder. But she had stopped struggling, and even if she had tried to make her feet move to get away from him, as his mouth returned to hers, she was not at all sure that they would have obeyed her.

'Are you sure you want me to?' he enquired, his voice laconic.

'Yes,' she said, but it was said only faintly, because she wasn't at all sure about anything any more, as ignoring her answer, his mouth once more claimed hers.

Alandra had been kissed only a few times before. But as Matt's mouth plundered hers and her arms of their

own volition acted independently of her and went up
and around him, she was soon learning that there were
kisses, and *kisses*!

And when Matt left plundering her mouth to bend
his head so he could kiss the swell of her breasts,
Alandra had by then no thought in her head that she
was behaving very oddly to feel this yearning need in
her for a man she hated.

She did not even recognise that things looked to be
getting out of hand when he pressed her yielding body
into him. Willingly, she pressed back.

But when he took his mouth from the upper swell of
her breasts, she was too far gone to notice that,
suddenly, he was still. That, suddenly, he was pulling
back from her. All that was in her mind then was that
soon she would feel his mouth over hers again.
Accordingly, she raised her face to his.

And then, if he had thrown the bucket of water over
her that she had promised him, Alandra could not have
been more shattered. Because he made no attempt to
kiss her again. It was as if he had found her far too
clinging, because he was taking hold of her hands and
removing her arms from his shoulders. And while she
stood passively, not even thinking of what happened
now, his harsh voice bit, was gravelly, and for long
seconds what he said left her stunned.

'So now we know.'

'Know . . .?' She didn't understand. 'Know—what?'

'Know that you *have* been in the nunnery far too
long.'

Nunnery! Comprehension was starting to dawn—and
suddenly, she was choking on it. 'You—you deliberately—set me up!' She could not believe it!

But she was having to believe it. It was there in his
harsh laugh. That laugh that held not a vestige of
humour. There in the mockery in his voice. And she
was back to hating him again. Hating the proof of her
question that was there in his answer:

'You're panting for sex—a bitch on heat wouldn't be so forward,' he tossed at her. And while she just stood and gasped, cuttingly he added, 'It was not my intention to help you out with *that* sort of succour. A thousand pounds is all you're getting—you'll have to look elsewhere for *that* kind of bonus.'

It was then that a fury entered Alandra's heart the like of which she had never before known. The night was black, but not as black as the hatred she felt for him just then. And as the fury in her went wild, so that deep blackness changed to a swift and sudden red, and that violent red was the only colour she could see.

And it was as if her swinging hand was guided by some homing device. For with perfect accuracy, it being too dark for him to see it coming, her hand arched through the air, and the cracking blow it caught him on the side of his face could not have been more satisfying to her.

'You've been asking for that for a long time now,' she spat at him viciously. 'Deduct *that* from the thousand!' And not waiting for anything, smartly she turned about and stormed indoors.

CHAPTER SEVEN

SHE awoke to find the world looking as sane and as normal as it had ever done. But as Alandra left her bed, there was none of the tremendous satisfaction in her that had been in her last night after she had taken that mighty swing at Matt Carstairs. She was feeling decidedly out of sorts this morning.

Alandra was not made to feel any better when, on going downstairs to breakfast, she discovered that everyone else seemed out of sorts too. Jo was for once already down, but if her glum expression was anything to go by, she had just been given short shrift by Matt.

But Alandra did not look at Matt as, not breaking with the tradition she had set, she muttered, 'Good morning.' The general response was less than enthusiastic. She reached for the coffee pot, but for the first time she ignored her habit of looking to see if anybody wanted a refill.

Robbie was looking ghastly, she noticed, determined not to go soft. Serve him right, she thought heartlessly, and pretended not to see the spaniel-eyed expression he attempted to throw her way, although hangdog, she mused, was more fitting this morning.

A clock somewhere struck the half hour and Robbie winced, and Matt got to his feet. Then Matt was leaving the room and Jo was chasing after him. Then Robbie was dragging himself to his feet and giving Alandra another shamefaced look, which she purposely didn't see, and he was following Jo out.

With just her and her grandfather left, she took her shoulderbag from where she had placed it on the floor, then removed from it the pearls she had worn the night before.

'Thank you very much for the loan of these,' she said, passing them over to him.

He looked at her, at the pearls, but he did not immediately put them into the natural repository of his cardigan pocket. Instead, gruffly he told her:

'I'd like you to have your grandmother's pearls, Alandra.'

But she was truly out of sorts that morning, and stubborn with it. 'Thank you, but I don't want them,' she said.

'My God!' he roared, snatching up the pearls and shoving them into his pocket, 'And they call *me* proud!'

'Good job he didn't do that while Robbie was still here,' said Jo, having made way for his charge past her as she came back into the room. 'Robbie's got a bad head,' she added, as she reached for the coffee pot.

'I had noticed,' said Alandra, still not feeling very sympathetic.

'Then you probably noticed too that Matt is ready to bite the head off anyone who says two words to him this morning,' said Jo, making Alandra wish she had taken a peek at him, if only to see if he was nursing a black eye—her hand still hurt from the blow.

'All because,' Jo went on to fume, when Alandra had thought she had finished, 'I dared to try and warn him that Corinne Hamilton will be angling for him again now that she's back.'

'Again?' she found herself asking, when in her view the dark-haired Corinne Hamilton didn't know how lucky she was if Matt Carstairs had escaped her the first time.

'She nearly had him hooked once, or thought she had,' Jo didn't hold back from telling her. 'But I thought when he threw her over and not long after she married some fat old man with fivers growing out of his ears, that Matt had chucked her because he had seen what an avaricious bitch she is.'

'She's married?' Again Alandra found herself asking

a question, when she was sure she wasn't in the least interested.

'Was,' said Jo flatly. 'It didn't take her long to wangle a divorce with a nice fat alimony settlement thrown in.'

'And you think she's come back to have another try for Matt?'

'Didn't you see her last night? She was all over him!' exclaimed Jo. But she did not wait for a reply, nor to finish the coffee she had poured. 'I'm going for a drive,' she said, though thought to ask just before she departed, 'Coming?'

Alandra shook her head. 'No, thanks,' she answered.

By mid-afternoon, having taken herself off for a long walk, Alandra was starting to feel in a much more sunny humour. Not that she regretted having served Matt Carstairs with that hefty swipe—it had been on its way to him for some time.

But it was such a lovely afternoon, and she decided not to think about him—or what, just by kissing her, he could do to her. She concentrated her thoughts instead on her blood relatives. She could have refused her grandfather's offer of the pearls more graciously, she thought, knowing that had she been in a better frame of mind—had Matt Carstairs and his belief that she was at Roseacres for what she could get not been there with her for most of the time—she could gently have told him her opinion that Jo, through her mother being her grandmother's only girl child, had more claim to the pearls.

Poor Jo, she mused, she had seemed to have forgotten about her crush on Matt—no accounting for tastes—when she had been dancing so happily with Jonathan Naseby.

And thinking of crushes, what was she going to do about Robbie? He had looked so crestfallen this morning when she couldn't raise a smile for him, she just knew he was feeling as miserable as he had looked.

Perhaps she should start making noises about leaving, but at that thought, she was suddenly filled with pain. She looked around, the view splendid, and her heart was caught. And she knew right then that, impossible as she sometimes found her relatives, and absolutely impossible as she *always* found Matt Carstairs, she did not want to leave.

Dressed in her robe that evening as she pondered on which of the dresses from her limited wardrobe she should wear at dinner, the thought she had had that Robbie was feeling as miserable as he had looked that morning was borne out when she answered a knock on her door and saw him standing there.

'C-can I see you privately, Alandra?' he quickly asked. And adding just as quickly when she looked to be going to say she would be in the drawing room shortly, 'I want to apologise for last night, and there's always somebody around downstairs.'

It was on the tip of her tongue to tell him 'So now you've apologised' and to close the door on him. But he looked so woebegone, and on reflection, for all her intentions had been for the best, she thought that maybe her behaviour at the ball had not, as Matt had said, been so well-mannered either.

'Come in, Robbie,' she invited. And at the first smile from her since he had disgraced himself, he came in and was again quickly apologising, revealing he had had a dressing down from Matt that day, Matt filling in the blanks he couldn't remember.

'I was horrified when Matt told me what I had said to you,' he said, a dull flush of colour coming up under his skin as he shook his head as if unable to believe it. 'I remember thinking with you so beautiful in your red dress that I wanted to—to cuddle you. So—I think that was all I meant when I said—what Matt said I said.'

He was really struggling, Alandra could see that, and her tender heart went out to her shy cousin who had been emboldened by alcohol. She was relenting fast when she smiled at him, for all she told him severely:

'Well—just you watch it in future.'

'Oh, I will,' he said eagerly. 'I'm sure I wouldn't have been so idiotic in the first place only . . .' he went red again, as he went on to say, 'only I think—I'm falling in love with you.'

'Oh, Robbie,' she said softly, and knew with regret that she was going to have to hurt him. 'There can be nothing between us.'

'Because we're cousins?' he asked, a maturity there in him that had thus far been hidden.

'I—just don't feel—that way—about you, Robbie,' she answered. And she knew that she never would feel 'that way' about him. She knew it even if there was no one else she was in love with either. A frown puckered her brow that with that thought, the face of Matt Carstairs should flash through her mind.

'You don't dislike me, do you?' he asked, banishing the unexpected picture of Matt from her mind. 'I know I'm not the brightest, and that I'm indecisive—you know I hate my job—yet haven't a clue what other sort of work I would like to do.'

'Many young men feel the same, I'm sure,' she told him, suddenly feeling years older than her earnest cousin. 'I've heard of many people changing jobs before they're thirty, and taking on entirely different careers from the ones they were trained for, purely because they had made a decision too early about what they wanted to do for the rest of their lives.' She smiled gently as she walked over to the door. 'It will come right for you, you'll see,' she assured him.

'And—you like me, Alandra?' he questioned, seeing she was opening the door, and going to stand in the doorway, but not looking ready to go until she had answered him.

She opened her mouth to tell him yes, that she did

like him. But a movement across the landing behind
Robbie had her eyes flicking quickly past his shoulder.
Oh, wouldn't you just know it, she thought as her eyes
met those of Matt Carstairs who had obviously been
just about to go into his apartment, but who had
stopped and half turned as he saw her open door.

It was the first time she had looked at him directly
since he had kissed her in the rose garden last night.
And it was to take a couple of seconds as she
remembered the feel of his mouth over hers and her
heady response, for her to get the memory out of her
mind, although not the memory of the comment he had
made about her being a bitch on heat.

'Do you, Alandra?'

She came to to realise that Robbie was almost
pleading with her to tell him that she liked him. Bitch
on heat, was she! Well, whatever Matt Carstairs thought
Robbie was doing in her room, she wasn't going to
disappoint him.

'I think you're super, Robbie,' she said. And smiling
tenderly at her intense cousin, she leaned forward and
kissed him gently on the mouth.

The sound of the door to Matt's apartment being
slammed shut reverberated through the whole house.
Though Robbie, looking star-struck, seemed not to
have heard it.

'That was just to show there are no hard feelings,' she
thought she had better tell him. He was still standing
there when she closed her door.

A more cheerful air prevailed over dinner that night.
For one thing, Jo appeared to have come to terms with
her panic that Corinne Hamilton had Matt in her sights
again. And Robbie, having shaken off his hangover and
discovered that Alandra thought him super, was in a
much more cheerful frame of mind. Matt too, for all he
had nothing to say to her, although she wasn't entirely
unaware of his eyes on her from time to time, seemed to
have succeeded in overcoming the temper that had had

him furiously slamming his door. He would doubtless consider she was leading her cousin on, she thought. And Grandfather Todd, she observed, didn't appear to be holding a grudge against her that she had refused to accept her grandmother's pearls.

In another five minutes, Alandra mused, they would all be going their separate ways, for the coffee had been poured and the meal almost over. Perhaps she would watch the play on T.V. that promised to be interesting. Matt seldom sat down to watch television. But, disgruntled to see that his face looked unmarked, not a sign of the black eye she had been hoping for, she would wait to discover what he was doing first.

'Would—would you like to come down to the pub for a drink tonight, Alandra?'

She turned to Robbie and catching Matt's narrowed-eyed gaze on her she was sorely tempted to accept. But she was saved having to find an excuse for not going when Jo butted in to state:

'I should think you had more than your share last night to last you a while.'

That he didn't like to be reminded, and that there was aggression in him she had not seen before, albeit only for his sister, was evident by the short way he replied:

'Well, Alandra can always drive me back if I get pickled.'

Sensing, as Jo's eyes sparkled, that the two might get started on an argument with Jo reminding him of what Matt had already filled in for him, Alandra thought she had better say something.

'Alandra doesn't drive,' she said. And saw her purpose had been achieved as Jo's eyes went wide.

'You don't drive!' she exlaimed, just as though she thought it was something one learned together with reading and writing.

Conscious that at Jo's exclamation all eyes had turned to her, Alandra was just about to say that they hadn't taught the subject at her school, when Robbie came in quickly to suggest: 'I'll teach you, Alandra.'

And while she was inwardly groaning, for Matt was looking as if he didn't like the idea at all, and she wasn't very keen herself she had to admit—visualising as she was the many hours tuition it would take, Robbie's declaration that he thought he was falling in love with her still bothering her—she heard her grandfather enter the conversation to state:

'Robert is a very good driver—you could do worse.'

As if to hear him compliment Robbie was something unheard of, both Jo and her brother turned their eyes to stare at their grandfather. But Alandra, when thinking Matt too would be looking at him, happened to glance his way, and she saw that Matt was looking at no one but her; the look in his eyes telling her that he had not yet forgotten seeing Robbie coming out of her room and that he didn't doubt that she had responded to Robbie in the same way in which she had responded to him last night.

She dragged her eyes from him to hear Robbie asking, 'Is that settled then, Alandra?'

From the soles of her feet, she found a smile, spirit in her determined not to be flattened by any look Matt cared to sear her with.

'According to Grandfather I could do worse,' she replied, and caught a glimpse of Matt pushing back his chair.

But her eyes were wholly on her grandfather and going wide with surprise, when she heard him offer, 'I'll buy you a car if you pass first time.'

Amazed by his generous offer, she became aware that though Matt was standing, he wasn't going anywhere. And she knew full well then that he would think it confirmation that she was here to take her grandfather for all she could get—if she agreed. She looked to the other end of the table, lifting her eyes to see a challenge in Matt's eyes—it was as if he was daring her to accept.

'Who——' she said, feeling her eyes held by his as though by some magnet so that she almost physically had to pull her eyes away, 'Who could resist such a challenge, Grandfather?'

Matt was at the door when Jo dared to ask him where he was going. 'Out,' was the short reply. But Jo's anxiety had her pressing, her voice sharp:

'Not with Lady Hamilton?'

For one dreadful moment, Alandra thought he was going to sink Jo without trace. The look in his eyes that anyone should dare to question his movements, said as much. But then suddenly, he smiled, though it was to her he was looking, and not at Jo, when he said:

'Unlike Horatio, I have two very good eyes.'

'Which means,' said Jo, happy all of a sudden as the door closed behind him, 'that Matt has seen through Corinne Hamilton.'

Alandra knew differently. Matt Carstairs hadn't been talking about Corinne Hamilton. What he had been saying, and he knew very well that she wouldn't have missed it, was that he had seen straight through Alandra Todd and her avaricious ways! Oh, how she wished she had blacked his eye!

On the way from the dining room, Alandra told Robbie she had decided to have an early night and would not be going to the pub with him. And having done herself out of the play she had been going to watch, she went early to her room, but only to discover, having felt tired from her long walk in the fresh air, that sleep was light years away.

Up early the next morning, she left going down to breakfast until she thought Matt and Robbie had gone. No point in looking for a fight to start the day, she thought. But she had for once forgotten that her watch gained ten minutes every day. And it was just her luck to reach the bottom of the stairs and to see Matt in the alcove where he must have stopped to answer the phone on his way out.

He looked to be going to put the phone on the rest, she saw, but as he noticed her about to pass, so he handed the instrument over.

'For me?' the question escaped her, when it was clear that it was. Feeling slightly foolish when he stood there impatient and not saying a word, sarcasm was her only ally. 'No doubt you asked who was calling,' she said, honey dripping.

She took the phone from him to hear not Hector, the only person she could think it was, but Frank Millington, the man Matt had cut in on at the ball. He was ringing early he said because he would be away for most of the day, and would she have dinner with him that night.

She didn't fancy the idea, though she didn't know why. Admittedly, she hardly knew him, but on the surface Frank Millington didn't appear all that bad.

'I . . .' she got as far as saying, her brain seizing up for an excuse with Matt there either waiting for Robbie—which must mean there was something wrong with Robbie's car, for they each drove themselves into Bedewick—or he was waiting to use the phone himself.

'I rang you about half past seven last night, actually,' Frank went on. 'But Matt said you were out.' And while her eyes shot to Matt who, looking as near a saint as he was ever likely to, looked back, 'Did he give you my message? I asked him to tell you to keep tonight free if it wasn't already booked.'

'Yes, Matt did give me your message,' she lied, partly in loyalty to Roseacres, partly because she thought Frank Millington was taking a bit much on himself telling her to keep tonight free. 'Can you hang on a minute?'

That imp of mischief had stirred. 'Tell me, Matt,' she said, placing her hand over the mouthpiece, 'is Frank Millington loaded?' The steel she had expected wasn't slow in entering his eyes.

'As Croesus,' he bit.

She considered his answer, Matt still wasn't going anywhere. 'Do you think a girl like me should dine with a man like him tonight?' she asked.

'You could *try* playing hard to get,' was his sarcastic suggestion. And having killed with that one sentence any sense of devilment in her, abruptly he turned about and went striding down the hall.

By the time Robbie, always first home, came in that evening, Alandra was sitting in the drawing room with a magazine, where she was beginning to wonder what the matter with her was that she should be so up one minute and down the next.

Perhaps she should have agreed to have gone out with Frank Millington, she thought. Perhaps she needed to be away from Roseacres and its occupants for a while. Perhaps she needed to be away generally to try and sort out what was bugging her.

'Alandra!'

She heard Robbie calling her name before he tried the drawing room and came in, a smile breaking on him to see her there.

'Ready for your first driving lesson?' he asked, looking the most buoyant she had ever seen him.

'Oh,' she said, having not given the matter any more thought. 'Don't I—er—have to have a provisional licence or something?'

'Damn—I forgot,' said Robbie, looking dismayed. 'I went out and bought some learner plates in my lunch hour, but I didn't . . .' His face cleared as he suddenly remembered something. 'There's a disused airfield not far from here. You don't need a licence to have a go there.'

Seeing it as a small thing to give in on in the face of the disappointment he would feel if she said no, Alandra agreed. And soon Robbie was happily driving with her as his passenger along winding country lanes and out to the disused airfield.

And, fair enough, he did give her some instruction,

and they did change places while she tried her skill at
the wheel. But when his hand lingered over hers far
longer than was necessary as, the car stationary, he
guided her hand to the reverse gear, she saw that if this
was how the lessons were going to continue, then
somehow she was going to have to put a stop to it, right
now.

'Alandra,' he said thickly, and turning to him she saw
that his face was much too close, and that he was going
to kiss her.

'No, Robbie,' she said, pulling back out of range. And
at the wounded look in his eyes, had to make herself go
on. 'Oh, Robbie,' she mourned, 'I'm fond of you—
cousinly fond. But it isn't any more than that.'

'But it might grow into something more,' he said
quickly, having taken heart that even if she wouldn't let
him kiss her, then at least she had admitted that she was
fond of him.

'No, No, it won't,' she replied just as quickly.

'How do you know? You're not giving it a chance
to . . .'

'I know, Robbie,' she said with conviction.

'Because you're in love with someone else!' he
exclaimed, reading from the conviction of her tone that
that must be the reason.

'I . . .' she said, and saw then that she had no choice
but to make him believe that. If she denied it, he would
not let up. That much had been proved because he had
returned to the subject when only last night she had
told him that there could be nothing between them.
'Yes,' she said, looking away from him. 'I am in love
with someone else.'

The journey back to Roseacres was a silent one,
Alandra cutting short Robbie's enquiry of just who she
was in love with, and his, 'He lives in London—this
chap?'

'Please, Robbie,' she had stopped him. 'It's—private.'

At the house she left him in the hall and went straight

to her room, feeling no happier than he had looked, at having had to resort to lying to him—even if it did mean that by doing so he seemed to have got the message that he should cease his attentions.

With half an hour to go before dinner, she thought she should do something about getting changed. But she had little appetite for dinner, and none at all for company.

Though it was company that she was to have. And she did not have to wait until she had joined everyone in the drawing room before she received that company either. Though perhaps the word 'receive' was not quite the right word. For when Matt Carstairs came bursting into her room, it was evident that he had not considered knocking and waiting to be invited.

And he wasted no time in sparking her defeated spirit into life, as much by his action in thinking it beneath him to knock on any of the doors in his house, as by the way, without preamble, he started to blaze into her:

'Where the hell have you been?'

About to angrily flare that she didn't care if it was his house, as a guest she was entitled to some privacy, she recalled the last time she had seen him with that same murderous light in his eyes. He was obviously stewed up about something—no point in inviting having her neck wrung.

'Good evening, Matt,' she replied as coolly as she could manage, a moment's panic in her at the way his nostrils flared at her sarcasm, and dousing the 'How nice of you to drop in' that would have followed. Though there was too much spirit in her to let him make a complete coward of her and she waved to the window, as she airily told him, 'If you would care to take a look at the drive, you'll see that Robbie has "L" plates on his car.'

Matt made no move to go and look out of the window, and that unexpected cowardice in her would have had her hiding under the bed had she not been able to control it as she saw it register with him that she had been with Robbie for a driving lesson. But that knowledge didn't appear to have taken anything away from his temper.

'Well, he can bloody well take them off again,' he bellowed, flattening the coward in her at being shouted at, making her mercury soar. But that was before he added, his voice only marginally less of a roar, 'I've arranged for you to be given professional lessons.'

'Professional le . . .!'

For blank seconds Alandra stared at him. And then, her ire cooled by his amazing announcement that *he* had arranged lessons for her, she discovered that not only was she capable of staying cool under the full threat of his anger, but that she was able to manage a sweetly false smile, as she asked:

'You're paying for my lessons, of course?'

'Who else?' he replied, the amount of lofty disdain in his voice leading her to believe that his initial fury was burning itself out.

'Ah,' she said, as suddenly she had the answer to why he had been so furious. Robbie hadn't been around when he had come home—neither had she. 'All this— your foul temper, your wanting someone else to teach me to drive—it's all because you think I might turn Robbie's head, isn't . . .'

'You've done that already,' he interrupted her aggressively.

'I . . .' She stopped, retaliation dying as she realised she hadn't a leg to stand on. And, for all she was hopeful that it was only a mini-crush her cousin had on her, her anger was subdued.

She was aware that Matt was still looking hostilely at her. Aware that he wasn't doubting that once she had her second wind she would come back at him. But suddenly, as the thought came that his concern for Robbie was bound up in him being brought up in the same house as her grandfather and her cousins, she discovered that she had nothing in her to let fly at him with. She felt flattened as it came to her that she was the odd one out. And further flattened as she realised that it should hurt that she was the one and only member of the Todd family whom Matt had no time for.

But there was no time then to analyse why that fact should hurt her so much. Time only to know that she felt wounded and just did not want to fight with him any more.

'You needn't worry about Robbie,' she told him tonelessly, relenting all at once when at any other time she would have been unable to suppress the urge to string him along. 'He knows he has no chance with me.'

'Oh sure,' Matt came biting back, his eyes narrowing as if he was trying to sort out what she was up to now. 'You showed him that by parting from him in the same affectionate way you parted from him when he left your room after his aperitif last night, did you?'

Perhaps that kiss to Robbie at her door before dinner last night had been a mistake, she thought, but she was glad of the stiffening that was coming to her at Matt's insulting remark.

'He only came to my room to apologise for his behaviour of the night before,' she said. 'He had no recollection of what he had said until *you* told him,' she thought to add. 'And,' she pressed, seeing that Matt, knowing Robbie as well as anyone, looked to be accepting that it would be like him to seek her out to apologise, 'I told him then that there could be nothing between us.'

She should have quit while she was ahead, she soon saw. For he was back to being belligerently aggressive at her last sentence.

'That was why you kissed him in such an un-cousinly way, was it?' he said, scorching her with a look. 'Just who are you trying to kid?'

Left without a leg to stand on again, Alandra bit her

lip. 'Well, I told him again not long ago,' she said defensively. 'He knows now, definitely, because . . .'

'Because?' he prompted when the words just wouldn't come. Though he did not look as if he was going to believe a word, whatever it was.

'Because,' she snapped, her anger poked into life again. 'Because I told him I was in love with someone else.'

He *wasn't* believing her, she could see that. In fact, she thought, noticing the way his jaw clenched, he looked astounded that not only should she say that she had told Robbie such a thing, but that he thought it incredible that she should ever be in love with anyone at all.

'That's not true,' he said, his tones harsh. 'You're lying.'

'No, I'm not,' she said, not quite sure which charge she was denying, but enough spirit back with her to have her not easily flattened again.

'You can't be in love with any . . .'

'My, my.' Thank goodness she was feeling more normal, she thought, as mockingly she interrupted him, that wild urge to string him along back to being her friend again. 'Now why would I turn my back on an eligible bachelor, even if he is my first cousin, if it wasn't that I was in love with somebody else?'

On the instant she finished speaking, Alandra knew that she had been far too cocky. She knew, without being terribly sure why, that Matt was looking murderous again, and that his control looked to be hanging by a very thin thread, and it was obvious that he wasn't liking her attitude.

But when he did move, and move quickly, he gave her no time to run. Grabbing hold of her arm he swung her round, and for her sin of telling lies, she knew that the thin thread of his control had just been split asunder.

'You lying bitch!' The words were grated at her as his

other hand came to take firm hold of her other arm. 'I know you're lying.'

And before she knew what he was going to do, though instinct was roaring at her that her cocky air had pushed him over the edge, just as though she weighed nothing at all, he had lifted her and had all but thrown her to the bed.

It was that same instinct that had her scrabbling to get to her feet. But she was not allowed to make it to more than a sitting position before Matt had joined her. And while her heart was going frantic with fear and lord knew what else, he was on the bed with her and was keeping her pinned to the mattress by the simple method of placing his body over the top of hers.

'We'll prove just what a little liar you are, Alandra Todd,' he growled. And she had not even begun to imagine what method he would use to get her to contradict what she had said, before she felt his mouth on her, burning, seeking, the way it had been that night of the ball.

Oh no! her senses shrieked, as firmly his body pressed into her and madly she began to struggle. Memory was with her of that time he had kissed her before. Memory of the way he had had her responding, when there had been no thought in her of responding! And she was afraid—afraid of herself.

Desperately she tried to get her hands free so that she could scratch and claw at him. But as his kiss deepened, and sought, and ravaged her mouth, it was all to no avail. She tried twisting her body, arching it against him, but only to find that that was a mistake. His body was not going anywhere but was pressing even closer to hers.

'No!' she cried, when still keeping her arms pinioned, his mouth left hers. Somehow he was able to drag her shirt back across her chest, his mouth doing a sortie to her throat and the swell of her breasts.

And it was there in her again, that same mysterious

wantonness possessing her as the buttons of her shirt came undone, and the material of her bra was pushed aside, and a warm mouth sought the fuller curve.

'No!' she said again, but to her ears it sounded more like a moan than the forceful 'No' it was meant to be.

His mouth hard on hers silenced any further protest. Yet, strangely, his hands were soft, gentle, as, her bra undone, she felt him cup her breasts and mould them.

'No,' she wanted to tell him. 'No. No.' But the caress of his hands on her was making her into a different person from the person she knew herself to be. Pink coloured her face as his mouth left hers and she saw his eyes go to where her breasts were exposed—but not one word of protest left her.

His mouth, the moist inside covering, caressing the hardened peak of her breast was doing mindless things to her. And when she arched her body to him a second time, there was just no thought in her head to try and twist away. She wanted to feel the hard pressure of him against her. Purely and simply, she wanted him.

'Matt,' she whispered, as her arms were released and his caressing fingers stroked her breasts as his mouth returned to hers. Her arms were holding him tight to her, when he broke his kiss.

'I . . .' she breathed, her eyes closed, not knowing where she was. 'Oh Matt . . .' she said huskily on a long shuddering sigh of wanting.

She guessed her cheeks were burning, the whole of her felt on fire. She knew Matt would not leave before he had taken this fever from her, until he had eased this terrible yearning, this longing in her he had stirred to life.

That was why, when expecting nothing less than that he would make her his, it was like a douche of ice-cold water to find that his hands had left her breasts and that he was moving—though not as she had supposed for some reason connected with the loving they would share—but because, for him, his aim had been achieved.

Her body felt cold when Matt did not immediately come back to her. And a smile of the delicious pleasure he had so far brought her was gentle on her mouth as she stretched sensuously.

Alandra opened her eyes, and saw that he was not doing anything other than standing at the bottom of the bed, his eyes cold as they swept up from her uncovered breasts and on to her face. Just to see him looking aloof from what she was feeling made a warning note sound in her head. But she was in no way prepared for the harsh words that came; harsh words that told her he had been playing with her for all the warm look of his skin revealed he had entered fully into the game.

'You respond to me like that yet reckon you're in love?' he sneered. And he was then moving abruptly to the door. Alandra lay staring transfixed as he turned and she heard that he had only one more sentence to say, 'Lady, you don't know the meaning of the word.'

The door was quietly opened and closed. And he was gone. Alandra let out a groan that was halfway towards being a sob. He was wrong, so wrong, she thought as she rolled over and buried her face in her pillow. She did know the meaning of the word. The meaning had been growing in her for some time now, only, obstinately, she had refused to acknowledge it.

Oh yes, she knew the meaning of that word love all right. And she was in love—she was in love with *him*!

CHAPTER EIGHT

How she got herself down to dinner and managed to be only a few minutes late, Alandra could not have said. Less than ever did she feel like eating. But, pride at stake, having been frozen into immobility at her earth-shaking discovery, that pride had stabbed at her and moved her into hurried activity.

She had no wish to dwell on Matt's lack of feeling for her, but knowing that he could treat her so carelessly as to arouse her to the pitch he had and then calmly walk out, had spirit mingling with pride that he should never know what else he had done to her.

'Sorry to be late,' she said brightly as she hurried into the dining room where everyone had just sat down. 'One loses all track of time when one's enjoying oneself.'

She was proud of her remark, even if she couldn't look at Matt. If he gathered from that that she could come from the soaring heights of his love-making and be untouched by it as if she had been standing at the kitchen sink peeling potatoes, then so much the better.

'You've been for your first driving lesson with Robert, I believe,' chipped in her grandfather. 'You enjoyed it that much?'

Oh grief, she thought, munching on thin toast and pâté, how the heck was she going to tell Robbie it had been her first and last lesson, when she had just given everyone—everyone save Matt, that was—the impression she had been thrilled to have been at the wheel of his car?

'As you said, Grandfather,' she replied, her mouth empty so she was unable to delay answering any longer, 'Robbie is a terrific driver.'

She was aware in turning to give Robbie a half smile that he was looking pleased, but she could not help that her eyes met Matt's stare full on. And she knew then from his arctic gaze that there was no thought in him of the time a short while ago when he had held her in his arms. There was cold fury about him only, she saw, as casually she let her eyes move from him—he thought that she was still leading Robbie on. And he would, she knew it, if she didn't get in first, announce to one and all that he had arranged for a professional to teach her.

'But, actually,' she said quickly, just getting in before him for there had been a deliberation about the way she caught a glimpse of him laying down his knife, 'I've . . .' Desperately she sought for invention, for tact, everyone was looking at her. 'I've remembered a friend of mine, who was taught to drive by—by a relation,' she made up. 'And they had awful rows as the driving lessons progressed. So,' she picked up her wine glass, and hoped she looked cooler than she felt as she took a sip, 'so I've decided, good teacher though Robbie is, that I don't want to learn to drive.'

And when Robbie came in immediately with, 'But . . .' not wanting an argument on the subject, she hurriedly cut him off, a touch of heat in her as she caught Matt's cynical cold-eyed look on her:

'There are one or two people of my acquaintance, Robbie,' she interrupted him, 'whom I wouldn't mind at all falling out with,' she wasn't looking at Matt, but he would know whom the cap fitted. 'But—but I should like to remain friends with you—if possible.'

That she was clearly telling Robbie that they could never be anything but friends, put the idea of arguing about giving her driving lessons out of his mind. And his only response to her was a gentle smile that made him the more endearing to her. And it was Jo who took up the question of someone else teaching her to drive, which had Alandra having to get in again quickly before Matt came out and said that it was all in hand.

'As a matter of fact,' she told her cousin, 'I've decided that I don't want to learn to drive at all.'

'But Grandfather was going to buy you a car if you passed first time!' exclaimed Jo.

Loving Matt, it surprised Alandra, having not noticed it before, how many times her eyes went to seek him out. Even while being determined not to look at him, she found her eyes going to him before she answered Jo. Hate for him came to confuse her as she read that look in his eyes that said 'Just what the hell are you up to now?' Defiantly she glared at him, then she turned quickly back to recall that Jo was waiting for a reply.

'I never was any good at passing exams the first time round,' she lied. And was ready to leave it at that. But it was her grandfather who came in then, a sudden if rare smile breaking across his frosty features, as quietly, he said:

'You're just like your father, Alandra.'

She looked at him, saw the traces of that smile still lingering, and a smile just as suddenly started in her. For whether her father had been any good at exams or not, she just knew that it was not that that he was referring to. What he was saying was that he knew, and unlike Matt, had seen that she, like her father, was just not interested in material acquisitions.

'Thank you, Grandfather,' she said, and was all at once feeling choked.

Knowing that she had been in an emotional state even before dinner, now that it was over and everyone was going their separate ways—her grandfather to his private sitting with his beloved pipe, Jo and Robbie to watch T.V., Matt, she observed, while pretending not to, making for the stairs—Alandra, like her grandfather, wanted to be alone. Not wanting to bump into Matt upstairs, she took herself off to the library and spent some time making believe she was going to select a book to read.

She took down a book at random, her mind too fidgety for any reading matter to make sense. She supposed for the look of the thing she had better pop her head in on Jo and Robbie to tell them she had got a good book before she went up to her room. And she was just leaving the library and passing near the front door when she bumped smack bang into Matt on his way out for the evening.

Regardless that her heart set up a wild beating that had her brain unable to think up anything very brilliant, she saw, in the interests of self-preservation, that she was honour bound to trot out something.

'Don't do anything I wouldn't do, Matt, dear,' she tossed airily at him, and wanted to groan at the inanity of her comment.

Guessing an acid backhander was coming her way, she didn't have long to wait as Matt favoured her with one of his arrogant stares:

'From what I've discovered about you and your ardent response to the most mild approaches from someone you wouldn't mind falling out with,' he charmingly told her, 'your remark gives me limitless scope—wouldn't you say?'

If he was waiting for her answer, he would have a long wait. Because with as much dignity as she could muster, no thought in her head that she had been going to say goodnight to Jo and Robbie, Alandra turned her back on him and went towards the staircase.

As anticipated, it was a complete waste of time taking a book with her upstairs to read. The first paragraph she thought she should know by heart, so many times did she read it. But not one word went in, so that in the end she put her book down and sat in unhappy thought until the time came when she should get into bed and, she hoped, shut out the world and all thought until the morning.

But, it was not to be. At midnight, Alandra got out of bed and put on her robe, thoughts of Matt out somewhere with the stunning Corinne Hamilton adding a new dimension to her unhappiness.

She tightened the belt of her robe and decided to go down to the kitchen and make a cup of tea. Lord knew what time Matt would come home—if he came home that night—jealousy turned like a knife. She had been awake for hours last night and had not heard him come in. He never came home early when he went out for the evening anyway—she wouldn't be at all surprised if he wasn't on first name terms with the milkman—so there wasn't the smallest likelihood of her sortie to the kitchen being interrupted.

Noiselessly she reached the kitchen, dark despair hers as she filled the kettle and put it to boil, then went to sit in one of the chairs at the kitchen table.

The kettle had a self-switch-off device which was fortunate because, an elbow on the table, Alandra sat in deep thought as she pushed her fingers through her hair and propped her head up, thoughts visiting and revisiting her troubled mind.

Oh, how could she be in love with such a man! As far as she could recall he had only ever been aggressive, rude and rough with her. Rough! Her thoughts took time off to recapture those wild moments in his arms. He had been harsh with her then as his mouth had ravaged hers. But rough! She recalled his hands, gentle, tender on her breasts; his lips, soft, caressing on her breasts. And suddenly—she was crying.

Matt hadn't been rough with her all the time. Some kisses he had bestowed on her had been lacking that savage quality that said he had been on the way to forgetting the forces that were driving him.

Her feeling of depression deepened. Her thoughts grew confused. And as the need to confide in someone smote her, so her tears fell faster. The only person she could have confided in was her dear sweet mother, and she was no longer there.

A sob escaped, its sound in the quietness of the

kitchen bringing her back to her surroundings. She made a move to get up from her chair, she would die of shame if Matt came home and found her with her spirit nowhere about her.

But Matt wouldn't be home, at least not for ages yet. Jealousy bit again as she imagined him with Corinne Hamilton, and as she thought of him staying out until the early hours—letting go of the control he had kept about him when he had been making love to her—so Alandra stayed where she was. And in the silent kitchen, she buried her head in her arms on the table, and cried her heart-break away.

Her head was still in her arms some ten minutes later, her ears deaf to all sound. And just as she had not heard the kettle click off when it had boiled, neither did she hear the kitchen door open.

So lost in misery was she, that she had no idea that a tall dark man had entered, his movements quiet so as not to disturb the sleeping household. For long moments his movement was stilled, the only sound the occasional faint murmur of anguish that came from the pale gold head caught in his glance over at the kitchen table. His jaw worked once, and then he moved.

It was a tremendous shock to Alandra's system when, in a world that had no room for outside noises, she heard the sound of the chair next to her being hooked back from the table.

'Well, well, poor Alandra,' said a voice she didn't believe she was hearing, sounding no more sympathetic than it had ever done. 'Just realising you were a shade hasty in your eagerness to thumb your nose at me, are you?'

Shock held her body rigid, and she would not look up. She had no idea what Matt was talking about, nor was she in a mind to try and decipher what could only be something disagreeable anyway. All she wanted was to be away from him to be back in her room. She couldn't bear that he should see her face awash with tears.

'Don't take it too hard, Alandra *dear*,' he continued to jibe, meeting no success if it was his intention to get her to raise her head. 'I'm sure you'll find some way of getting your grandfather to come across in either cash or kind.'

Tears dried as she comprehended that he thought she was heart-broken because she had overplayed her hand and deprived herself of a brand new car. But still she didn't move. Her tears now felt cold on her face, but pride was preventing her from putting up a hand to wipe them away while he was watching.

'Or is it that you're having second thoughts about the wisdom of playing hard to get where the wealthy Frank Millington is concerned?' he continued, and would have said more. Only at that moment, Alandra had heard more than she could take.

Vaguely she was aware that Matt was not giving credence to the fact that she was genuinely upset. In all probability he was thinking she had some plan in mind to be in the kitchen putting on an act for when he came home. But the knowledge that he must think her the most scheming, conniving hussy of all time, was more than she could take. Hiding her face, fresh tears flowing from her eyes, suddenly Alandra rocketed from her chair and went streaking for the door.

But too soon she learnt that Matt's look of fitness was no false promise. Because with a turn of speed that outmatched hers, he too was out of his chair, and he was at the door before her. And he was not, she discovered as she kept her head bent, in a mind to let her run away.

Holding her firmly by one arm, he turned her, his other hand coming to force her chin up. And as she heard his jerked grunt of an exclamation, she knew he had seen for himself that she was not shamming her obvious distress.

Her pride in ashes that anyone should catch her

weeping, she tried to get free. But he was refusing to let her go, though there was still no sympathy thats he could detect when he said in that granite voice he had used all along:

'What's this? Tears—real tears—from a hard case like you?'

Unable to answer him, desperately she tried to get her scattered wits together. Ashamed of her damp face, she sought and found her handkerchief in the pocket of her robe, and made a hasty, though futile attempt to mop away all traces of tears.

She made an immense effort to get herself together, but it was difficult with Matt still holding on to her arm. And a long shuddering breath left her, as endeavouring to get somewhere near to top form, she found her voice.

'W-would you believe,' she said, her voice all husky and not her voice at all as she looked anywhere but at him, 'that—that I've—been peeling onions?'

She tried to smile, but it didn't come off. And then as Matt shook his head slowly from one side to the other, she had to look at him.

He had sounded rock hard and tough when she had not been looking at him. But as her eyes met his, even if it was only a fleeting second before she looked away, she could have sworn she had seen a spark of admiration there that she was a fighter still.

'No—I wouldn't believe,' he confirmed the shake of his head. 'Not for a minute.'

'Oh,' she said, and was stumped, her powers of invention dried as her tears were drying. Yet Matt didn't look to be ready to let her go until he had found the reason for her 'real' tears.

'Why not try the truth?' he suggested.

Conscious that his eyes had never left her face, Alandra's mind was a blank. Feverishly her eyes moved round the kitchen, then stopped when they caught sight of the kettle she had put to boil.

'I—couldn't sleep,' she said, the truth only available since nothing else was presenting itself. 'I—came down to make m-myself a cup of tea.'

Had she been hopeful that that would be a sufficient explanation, then as she tried to turn for the door and the hand on her arm gripped more tightly, she realised she should have guessed that Matt would not let her get away with it.

'You always break down when you can't sleep?' he enquired, and his voice was even now, so that she dared a look at him. But only to find her eyes pinned by his. Quickly she looked away. Aside from hating anyone to see her in tears, she just knew she was looking a mess, her pale hair all tumbled anyhow from having her fingers pushed through it, her eyes damp still.

'I think I shall be able to sleep now,' she said, and tried again to pull from his hold, and met as much success as she had before.

'Did you have your tea?'

His enquiry threw her. So did the way he pulled her back from the door. She watched his eyes flick around for her used cup and saucer, and knew then since he was showing no sign of letting her go—not without an undignified struggle which she just wasn't up to—that she needed time to piece some falsehood together which might be acceptable.

'Would you like some tea?' came blurting from her. Surely in the time it took to make it, she could think of something other than that she had been breaking her heart over him! And he must have come into the kitchen for something, she thought. Though of course it could be that as last one in, he had come to check that the house was secure for the night.

Her answer was to be that he led her back to the chair from which she had so rapidly bolted. And, unbelievably, to her mind, his voice was not unkind when he told her to, 'Sit there,' and had to exert only small pressure to have her doing just that. For whether it was surprise that his voice suddenly held no aggression for her, or whether it was because she had exhausted herself, she did not know, but her limbs felt weak and she was glad to have the chair beneath her.

When he left her to go over to the kettle, and took down two cups and saucers, fresh surprise kept her seated. By the look of it, not only was he going to join her in a cup of tea—but he was going to make it!

The kettle did not take long to boil. And there were no further questions coming from Matt while he waited for the tea to brew. Which caused her to think, oddly— could it be that he was giving her this little time to get over her shock of finding she was not as alone as she had been certain she would be?

But when the tea was brought over and he came to sit next to her, she was to realise that those minutes she had been looking forward to having in which to concoct some suitable lie, had all been spent in thinking of him. And that she had not come up with even the tiniest fib as an excuse for why she had been indulging in a jolly good howl when he had come in and caught her at it.

She fiddled with the cup and saucer he had placed before her, but still was not ready with an answer, when, his voice still even, pleasant almost if her whole system wasn't so shot her ears were picking up nuances that weren't there, he said thoughtfully:

'Do you know, Alandra—I'm beginning to think you're not such a hard case after all.'

And panic was all hers then. The last thing she wanted was that he should start to re-think anything about her! Who knew, with the intelligence that lay behind his clever eyes, he might even root out that she had been sobbing so bitterly because she had been such an idiot as to have fallen in love with him.

Now more than ever she needed her pride. Now more than ever she needed to be the hard case he thought her. Though he would never know the effort it cost her to rouse herself to retort, 'Don't do me any favours.'

Though, she had to admit, it wasn't much of an effort, for her voice was still husky and lacking in the sharpness she had wanted.

She tried again, feeling the need to excuse her tears. But in so doing, had Matt been setting a trap for her, then obligingly, she fell headlong into it, when with as much sharpness as she could muster, she belligerently told him:

'I didn't expect you home yet. I wouldn't have . . .'

'You wouldn't have let me or anyone else see you in tears,' he cut in with sharp discernment. 'Am I not right?'

Having just used up what small supply of aggression she had, Alandra did not answer. She felt too vulnerable just then to say a single word that might confirm in any way that she was far from being the hard case he thought her, that he might be right to be having minute second thoughts. She felt no match for him just then, and could not think of one snappy reply to come back with. Far better, she thought, for her to go straight up to her room. By tomorrow she would be on an even keel again.

But—yet—she did not want to go. She had to admit that even while owning that she must be all over the place. This was the first time she had said more than two words to Matt without his aggression being out in full force. And, greedy though it might be—doing herself no good as it might be—she wanted just a few more minutes with him being the nearest to being kind to her that he had ever been.

'Drink your tea,' he instructed, when his had been dispensed with and hers was going cold.

She took one or two sips, and fought a silent argument within herself. Common sense very nearly won, and she was just about to short cut any questions he had on her blubbering and say a brief goodnight then go to her room, when Matt said, and there *was* kindness in his voice, defeating her will to leave:

'Are you now ready to tell me why those beautiful green eyes have been drenched by tears?'

With him sitting so near, he could have stopped any movement she made to go to her room by the simple expedient of putting out his hand. And that was why, she told herself, she made no move to go. But no way was she going to tell him what he wanted to know. Although she had a dreadful feeling that, having found something that didn't quite tie up—the impression he had of her to date being that she was too much of a tough nut ever to cry real tears—then Matt was just not the sort who would let go until he had got to the bottom of it.

'You think my eyes are beautiful?' she asked in an attempt to throw him off course, not wanting that a tiny glow should come to further confuse her thinking.

'Trying to side-track me, Alandra?' he replied, showing he was more than up to her tricks, if she didn't already know it.

'Were you always this smart?' she tried again.

'I don't think anyone would have to be too bright to know that you have been having some very unhappy thoughts,' he out-smarted her, too easily bringing the conversation back round to why she had been crying. 'What thoughts were going through your head when I came in?'

Wild horses, plus, would not have had her telling him a word about it being the new discovery of her love for him that had battered at the outer covering she showed the world. Never would he hear from her that the way he usually was with her had had her in dark despair, that that wasn't the way she wanted him to be with her. He would probably fall off his chair if she so much as mentioned that in imagining him making love to Corinne Hamilton, kissing her so soon after he had had her melting in his arms, had had jealousy tearing her emotions to shreds.

But Matt was waiting. Waiting, not saying another

word, as silently he gave her more time to get herself
together. But Alandra was nowhere near to getting
herself together, jealousy of Corinne Hamilton renewing
an attack even though Matt was now with her.

'I was—thinking about ...' she halted, memory
returning of how her tears for her hopeless love for him
had been mingled with tears for her mother who was
not there for her to confide in.

'About what?' he asked, so very quietly, and it was
almost as if he really cared that anything should make
her unhappy while she was under his roof.

Tears came near to the surface that her imagination,
vivid when thinking of him with Corinne Hamilton,
could not have dimmed any because it was now
allowing her to imagine that there was some caring in
Matt for her.

'I was—thinking about my mother,' she told him, her
voice subdued. 'My mother died recently.'

'How recently?'

Had she imagined also that a sharper note had come
to his voice? Did he think she was lying; that she would
lie over a thing like that? Whether his voice had an edge
to it or not, Alandra was suddenly stiffening, and her
voice had a definite edge of its own, when she replied:

'Just over two months ago.'

A moment's pause and he was asking, 'Your
mother's death upset you—you were fond of her?'

Hearing only that he must think her some kind of
monster to question if she had been upset, Alandra
missed hearing that his question had been on the gentle
side.

'Are you fond of your mother?' she asked, aggression
stirring.

Her aggression was ignored, his voice thoughtful as
he asked, nothing wrong with his mental arithmetic,
'You came to Roseacres a month after your mother's
death—was that because, upset as I believe you were,
you felt a need to be near your family?'

Her eyes flew to his face, love she was discovering could have you down in the depths one minute and sailing over Everest the next. Just by that simple statement that he believed she had been upset, joy had quickly trampled on depression. But with Matt looking sincerely back at her, she found it impossible to lie to him. Even while knowing that to deny she had felt a need for her family would endorse for him that she had arrived when she had purely because she had read of her grandfather selling out to him, she could not lie to him.

'No,' she said, and carried on as his lips firmed at her answer, 'I felt no need to see any of my father's family.'

His look was direct as he filed away her reply. And Alandra thought that now he certainly wouldn't raise any objection to her returning to her room. He had discovered that her tears were on account of her recently losing a loved mother, and in consequence had had it confirmed that he had been right all along to think that her only purpose in coming to Roseacres was for what she could get out of her grandfather.

Pride asserted itself, and with the intention of leaving him, she went to rise from her chair. But then she found as his hand came out and stayed her, that apparently Matt did not consider he had heard all that he wanted to hear.

Because she had no choice, Alandra subsided into her seat, but she determined then, as with his aim achieved he withdrew his hand, that not one word of her promise to her mother, or that letter her grandfather had written, would he hear from her if he was bent on dissecting her reasons for calling that day.

But to her surprise, although since he had been sure before and now she had just confirmed it, maybe he didn't consider pursuing the matter necessary, because he did not question why he and her grandfather should have come home that Saturday and found her there. Though his question when it came was to make her wary as she discerned that Matt, having discovered her when her defences were down, was taking advantage of the one and only time she had shown any weakness to get a further insight into her and the life she had led before that Saturday.

'Alain told me that your mother was delicate as a young woman,' he began. 'Was it always so?'

'She never got any stronger, if that's what you mean,' she answered carefully.

'There were days when she was—more delicate than others?'

'It wasn't her fault if that's what you're getting at,' she answered tartly, protective still of her mother. 'She should never have had me, but she insisted on . . .'

'That *wasn't* what I was getting at,' he interrupted mildly. Which had her looking at him and forgetting for the moment to be wary. 'You were frequently hard pressed, so you've said. Which makes it unlikely, I think, for you to have been able to afford the services of a nurse. It occurred to me to wonder, who then looked after your mother when she required nursing?'

'My father,' she replied without hesitation. 'That was why we were nearly always broke.' And in case he had anything sour to say about her father, 'He had his priorities right you see. My mother's well-being came before any job with a chance of promotion.'

'He was often away from his work?'

'More often he changed his work—most employers are more interested in workers who can guarantee a smooth-flowing output—few will stand the disruption to that flow, even if they sympathise with any employee who has to continually take time off.'

'Your father died six years ago?' Alandra nodded. Matt had known that anyway, so she couldn't quite see the point of his question. That was until he asked, 'Who looked after your mother when he died—you were only fourteen then?'

'We managed,' she answered, leaving him to guess that there were days when she had not gone to school.

'Did you frequently change employers too?'

Alandra thought of Hector Nolan, and smiled. 'I was more fortunate than my father. I had a very understanding employer.'

Her mind was still on Hector and how kind he had been, not only in letting her have the flat, but not minding her leaving her work so she could dash upstairs to check on her mother, so that she wasn't prepared for the question that came smoothly:

'Your employer was so understanding that you threw your job up?'

'I—had to,' she replied.

'Because?' His voice had hardened, and it nettled her into answering sharply.

'I wasn't caught making off with the profits, if that's what you would love to know.' And, her anger going as quickly as it had come, her voice faltering as she remembered, 'When—when I knew that my—mother's time was—limited, I—I wanted to be with her as much as I could.' Memory was bright, the surrounding kitchen fading, as gone from him, she recalled, 'Poor, poor darling, she'd had enough of hospitals, I wanted to nurse her myself.'

The hand that came gently over hers brought her back to the kitchen at Roseacres. Though it was for some seconds that she stared into dark eyes that were suddenly showing a sensitivity she had never before seen.

'That must have been hard for you,' he said quietly, seeming to know, she thought, that the hardest part had not been the work involved, but that of being helpless to stop the deterioration in the mother she had loved.

She swallowed, and then gulped, and was fighting hard to keep tears at bay, as her voice choky, she told him, 'If this—if this little—chat—was designed to send me to bed less tearful, then you're not doing a very good job.'

Matt's sudden smile went a long way to help her over the weakness that threatened. How it lightened his face, made him more approachable. To see his mouth pick up at the corners, even if his smile was a shade rueful that, though he didn't know it, for the second time that evening, tears were ready, and he the cause of stirring them.

Then his smile had gone as quickly he edged the subject out of prime place. 'This man, the one you think you're in love with,' he said, his tone mild but not the look of him as a frown accompanied his words, 'with you being so busy nursing what time did you have for him?'

Knowing the ground she was on had suddenly become shaky, abruptly she turned her face so that Matt couldn't see into her eyes.

'I—found time,' she managed to lie after a struggle. But she did not have to lie at his next question.

'Did he live with you?'

'No!' Her answer was out, sharp and denying, before she had given herself time to think about it.

'That was positive enough,' he said, but hadn't finished with his questions she discovered, when he asked, 'But you and he were lovers?'

Badly she wanted to say 'yes'. She had no idea at all why Matt had started on this tack. It might have been just idle curiosity, and must be that, she thought, for she could not think of any other reason for his question.

'As a matter of fact,' she said, and lost the 'yes' she had been after when suddenly his hand came to take her chin and he turned her face so he should read the truth in her eyes. 'As a matter of fact ...' she repeated, and swallowed as she tried to get the lie out. A lie she was to find that just would not come, not with his eyes fixed on hers it would not. 'No,' she said.

'But,' his face was stern, his hold on her chin firm, as

not letting up, he pressed, 'But there have been lovers, Alandra?'

'You're—you're g-getting too—personal,' she said, and had wrenched her chin out of his hold, and was on her feet ready to run for the door.

She didn't make more than two steps forward before he had caught her. Caught and held her, his arms coming round her, defeating her moment of strength to run from him.

Alandra gave in. The stuffing had gone out of her. And when Matt pulled her closer, though his hold on her was not tight, weakly she allowed her head to rest on his shoulder for sanctuary-giving moments.

'From the way you were on your bed tonight, I think I have leave to believe you didn't think me too personal then,' he said, his voice very near to her ear.

'Don't, Matt,' she whispered. 'I think—you're aware now, that—I don't know all the rules to that little game you were playing with me up in my room.'

She raised her head then, realising that this was insane, that he should let her go. Tomorrow he would have forgotten this interlude—she never would.

His grip on her tightened briefly. 'I don't think you know *any* of the rules, do you, Alandra?' he asked softly. And gently then he kissed her brow. 'That certain—naïvety in your response to me on that bed had me thinking it was part of your holding back; part of the same way you were struggling to get away from me to start with. But it wasn't that was it? Somehow I had managed to trigger off that fire of passion in you, and while after a tussle you were eager to make love— you just didn't have a clue what you were supposed to do, did you?'

That he had no idea how he had triggered off that passion in her, though in her view he was expert enough without her learning after that her love for him had been the trigger, meant she thought, that he could not have seen that her love for him would deny him nothing.

'Please, Matt,' she begged. 'Don't dissect it. You—were mad at me. And I—I have never met anyone with your experience before—c-can't we leave it at that?'

He looked down into her appealing green eyes. Eyes that showed their recent grief. And whether it was because of what she had told him had been the cause of her grieving, she didn't know, but a gentler note was added to his voice as he said:

'You're tired. Will you be able to sleep now if I let you go?'

Awash with relief, shyly she smiled up at him. 'Yes,' she said softly.

And she was then in heaven. For Matt's head had come down and his lips were on hers. And it was such a gentle kiss, lingering and not harsh. And as her heart started to beat a staccato beat, Alandra knew she would have done anything he asked of her then.

But Matt was asking nothing from her, for all that rueful smile was back with him again and abruptly he put her from him.

'Go to bed, Alandra,' he said, but added as she moved from him, 'while—I can let you.'

CHAPTER NINE

AT half past six Alandra awakened, and as memory surged in, there was not the smallest chance of her going back to sleep.

That her love for Matt had had her going so soft that she had gone to pieces downstairs in the kitchen last night, seemed, in the cold light of day, only marginally less incredible than that he had shown her a kindness never before seen in him. And just as incredible was the fact that he had been on the point of re-thinking his opinion of her.

But, with part of her wanting him to see she was not the hard case he had up until last night believed her, she was tormented for the next half an hour by frightening thoughts that if he continued in the same vein in which they had parted—a suggestion there that he had wanted to do more than comfort her with just one gentle kiss— then wasn't she in danger of going soft on him again; of drooling all over him!

Hastily she got out of bed and hurried to get bathed and dressed. But she was chased the whole time by the thought that if she didn't do something about it, Matt was going to know before very long that she had fallen heart and soul in love with him!

Anguished thoughts still with her, she recalled the affectionately indulgent way Matt treated Jo, and the way Jo's eyes followed him wherever he went. Not that he would treat her so indulgently, her pride wouldn't stand for it in any case, but ... Unable to stay in her room any longer, her mind in turmoil, Alandra went silently down the stairs, the realisation with her that now more than ever did she need to get away to straighten out her thinking.

Her mind hopping all over the place, Matt the nucleus, she almost missed seeing her grandfather coming along the hall from the opposite direction.

'Walk through me,' he grunted.

'Er—Good morning, Grandfather,' she said, forcing her thoughts away from their central point. 'No rose garden this morning?'

'I'm just going to get my pipe,' he replied, and would have gone on to his sitting room, only the words spilling from Alandra had him halting to study her.

'I think I'll go to London for the day,' she said, the thought that had barely had time to take root in her mind, out before she could think further.

'Sudden decision, wasn't it?'

'You know women, Grandfather,' she returned lightly.

'Come and tell me about it,' he said. And because he was moving to his sitting room, no thought in his head that she wasn't behind him, Alandra followed. Though to her mind, there was nothing to tell.

But it was in his sitting room, sensitive that no one should guess her need to be away from Roseacres, that she dreamt up an excuse for taking an early train from Ferny Druffield, when at any other time she would not have thought an excuse necessary.

'The shops in Bedewick are quite good,' she told him, 'but I'm better acquainted with the shops in London, and I know exactly where to get the things I want there.'

'So you're going on a shopping spree!' he remarked, moving from her to open a drawer in his writing desk.

Alandra saw him withdraw a dilapidated old cash box, but paid little heed as she went on to elaborate that she had good reason to spend a day in London.

'Not only that,' she said, 'I haven't seen my friends in ages, they'll think I've emigrat . . .' Alain Todd pushing a bundle of five-pound notes into her hands had her breaking off to exclaim, 'What's this?'

'You'll be needing a few coppers if you're going shopping,' he said, his look brooking no refusal.

'Coppers!' she exclaimed, looking at the wad of notes, and trying to push them back at him. 'I don't want your money, Grandfather,' she said severely as he refused to take it, as determined he should take the money back as he was determined that he would not.

'Neither did you want your grandmother's pearls,' he said, making her brow pucker at the thought she had really hurt him over that. 'Nor did you want the car I would have bought for you no matter how many tries you had at passing a test,' he added. About to interrupt to gently remind him that she had let him pay for her ball gown, he dented her compunction further, as looking saddened, a sigh he couldn't hold back leaving him, he went on, 'Am I not allowed to have pride, too, Alandra?'

'Grandfather, I . . .'

'Want nothing from me,' he interrupted, shaking his head sorrowfully.

'Oh, Grandfather,' she said helplessly, 'I . . .'

'Have you been unhappy here?' he asked, turning ponderously away, taking her mind from the money she still held in her hand as he went to close the cash box and put it back in the desk drawer.

'I—stayed, didn't I?' she answered. Which seemed to be enough of an answer for him, for suddenly as he turned, his rare smile came out, and he was saying simply:

'I'm glad you did. I enjoy your being here, Alandra.' And she knew that he meant it, as she wondered why his confessing that should make her feel weepy again. He then cleared his throat, and said quietly, 'You've done my heart good, child.'

Her feeling of wanting to weep was buried under the gentle smile that came to her. She guessed it had not been easy for him to come out with that.

'And now, if we don't want Mrs Pinder chasing us

up, we had better get to the breakfast table,' he said gruffly. And he had the door open for her to go through before he remembered why he had been making tracks for his sitting room in the first place. 'My pipe,' he said as she moved through the doorway.

But she moved not another step. For it was then, as he went back to hunt up his pipe—a pleased smile still on her face from his remark that she had done his heart good—that she saw Matt coming along the hall not ten yards away.

Lost for anything to say as he drew level, and halted, her face went pink from just seeing him. But as he took in the pleased look of her, and she saw his eyes go down to her hands, Alandra's face fairly flamed. For only then did she realise that she was still holding the money her grandfather had thrust at her!

She kept her eyes on her hands, it obvious to her then that Matt, too, having woken to the cold light of day, had put behind him any second thoughts he might have had last night about her not being such a hard case. How could he not? There was blatant evidence in her hands that deprive herself of a brand new car she might have done, but as he had suspected, she had got up early this morning to—as he had put it last night—get her grandfather to come across with either cash or kind.

She wasn't even capable of wishing him good morning. Her grandfather appeared behind her as she thrust the money out of sight and into her trousers pocket and led the way into the breakfast room. She knew she had been looking as guilty as hell, just as she knew that there wasn't a thing she could do to absolve herself if Matt wasn't to use his discernment to probe— as he would. But why, suddenly, was she bothered about what he thought, when she never had before?

She had verification that he had lost all sign of the empathy that had been with him late last night. Because there was not a kindly nuance about him this morning when, after both men had partaken of the coffee she had poured, her grandfather saw no reason why Matt should not be told she was going to London.

'What are you going to London for?' he bit, regardless that her grandfather was observing with mild interest.

'Do I have to have a reason?' she snapped, glad to find she was still capable of firing up at him, and not as she had been beginning to suspect, made a paler shadow of herself through love of him. He ignored her question, his bark only fractionally more civilised.

'When are you coming back?'

That he was looking to be civilised at all had her fire cooling. Though she had to count a few digits before she was sure she had the honeyed tones she wanted.

'Before you'll have missed me, I'm sure, Matt dear,' she said sarcastically. But she only succeeded in wounding herself with the truth of the remark, for it bounced off him, as he said, as though he couldn't wait to be rid of her:

'I'll take you to the station.'

'Don't put yourself out on my account,' she told him, waspish in her hurt. And was glad then to find that her mischievous impulses hadn't deserted her either. 'I can always go up and get Robbie out of bed . . .'

Matt killed her with a look. 'Be ready at twenty to eight,' he rapped.

She ignored him. 'More coffee, Grandfather?' she offered.

At twenty to eight precisely, Alandra presented herself on the drive. Matt's face couldn't have been colder if he had spent the night in the deep-freeze, she considered as she got into his car beside him. Barely had she closed the door then he was pulling away, another indication, she thought, determined not to let him see that it bothered her, that Matt Carstairs wanted to be rid of her.

Although not, she was to hear, before he had reminded her of the thousand pounds he had promised to pay her for staying at Roseacres for three months.

'That deal we made,' he said, sounding every bit as cantankerous as her grandfather on occasions, 'is only valid providing you spend every night of those three months under the roof of Roseacres.'

'*Now* he tells me!' she jibed.

'You come back tonight, or the deal is off,' he told her in no uncertain terms.

Sorely wanting to tell him what he could do with his thousand pounds, she thought better of it. 'Even Cinderella was allowed out until midnight,' she replied instead.

The next mile was covered with Matt maintaining a morose silence. But he hadn't finished having a go at her, she discovered. Although she could have wished he had chosen to refer to anything other than the mad reckless way she had reacted to his kisses.

'Perhaps it was a mistake to have let you go to bed after only one kiss last night,' he said, his voice suddenly silky, so that already wilting at his choice of conversation pieces, Alandra just knew she was in for some of his not-too-pleasant sarcasm. 'I should have realised from the hot way you've reacted to me on more than one occasion, that being shut away at Roseacres has left you starved for a man's kisses.'

She gripped tight on to her bag in her lap, that or crown him with it. It was apparent that he thought she was going to London to see the man she had told him she was in love with.

'Just practising, Matt dear,' she said as coolly as she could, not missing the way his jaw clenched when she added, 'But at the risk of hurting your feelings, I think you should know that some kisses are *more* special than others.'

Alandra wouldn't have been surprised to see icicles hanging from the interior of the car as Matt banged from it at the station yard, and she followed suit.

It was touch and go whether she blew up at him, when refusing to move over he presented himself at the glass window of the ticket office, her friend the station master now ticket issuer-in-chief, and would not let her pay for her ticket.

'First-class day return to London,' she heard him state. And couldn't help wondering how she could on the one hand love him so much, yet on the other, wish that she was wearing steel toe-caps so that she could give his ankle a crack.

'There's a train back at ten past six,' Matt informed her, his silkiness gone as he walked on to the platform and handed her ticket over. 'Be on it.'

She had only time to say a sugared, 'You hadn't better meet me in case I miss it—I just couldn't bear to see you cross,' then he had gone.

There had been time on her journey for her to do some of the thinking she had come away from Roseacres to do. But all that went on in her brain on that journey, and during her taxi ride to her flat, were thoughts of Matt. Snatches of last night and the way he had been, coming back to her. And, more recently, memory of the taciturn man who had driven her to the station filled her mind.

At her flat, she opened windows to give it an airing, then sat down to think. Only to find that she was wasting more time. Without knowing it she had got up and had begun pacing her flat, trying to decide what she should do. Impossible, she thought, to do nothing.

Hector Nolan ringing her doorbell just after one had her coming out of her reverie where she was again folded in Matt's gentle arms of the night before.

'Thought it must be either you or mice with clogs on,' said Hector, coming into her apartment above his office. 'Are you going to be an angel and tell me that you're back for good and are just about to go to the Jobcentre?'

'As bad as that?' she asked, pleased to see Hector,

though she would have popped in to see him had he not called up.

'Your replacement didn't even work out her month's notice,' he complained. 'She said it wasn't necessary as she hadn't been with me long enough. They've got you all ways these days,' he added, then went on, 'Come back, Alandra,' and rashly, 'You can name your salary.'

The words, 'With an offer like that, who could refuse?' were out, and could not, in the face of the delighted smile that widened his mouth, be drawn back.

He took her out to lunch, and Alandra, a decision made, was left wondering had it been a conscious decision? Had she meant all along to see Hector about having her job back? She couldn't be sure, but as she sat in the train on the way back to Roseacres, she was glad of one thing at least—she had ceased dithering.

But that was all she had cause to be glad about. Soon she would leave Roseacres, and never would she see Matt again. She knew she was going to feel pain for some time about that. And her heart pumped painfully when alighting from the train, because there was Matt to meet her.

He did not ask if she had had a good day, and seemed as morose as he had been that morning. She had not one parcel with her, so she guessed he was thinking, had her grandfather related her excuse of a shopping trip, that his surmise was right and that she had been to London to see her man-friend.

Matt didn't beat about the bush either, and was obviously looking for confirmation when he asked, 'Did you see him?' He sounded tough as he started up the car.

'Is it likely that I'd go to London and not see him?' she answered, not pretending she didn't know what he was talking about.

In no time, as he put his foot to the floor and accelerated, they were at Roseacres. And if the thought had touched down that the furious way he had driven was because he did not like the idea of her going to London to meet some man, then she very soon saw just how utterly ridiculous she was being to allow herself such fantasy of thought.

For once at Roseacres, barely giving her time to get out of the car, Matt was swinging the vehicle around, and was driving just as furiously back the way he had come.

Her thoughts that he had a date, and that meeting her train had caused him to cut it fine, were soon to be borne out when, with only minutes to spare before dinner, she made it to the drawing room. But she found that she need not have rushed because Jo was the only one down.

'I'd have come to London with you had I known you were going,' she said, looking as depressed as Alandra felt as she complained that her grandfather had been in a foul mood all day, and that Robbie had worn a face as long as a fiddle ever since he had learned he wouldn't see her until later that evening. 'Did Matt meet you at the station all right?' she thought to enquire at the end.

'He—seemed in a hurry,' Alandra murmured, thinking all the men at Roseacres were wearing the same hat by the sound of it.

'He's just as bad,' said Jo moodily. 'I hope that Corinne Hamilton puts him in a better frame of mind.'

So he did have a date! Alandra thought, and speared by jealousy she knew then that she was right to leave.

'All I said to him was that I bet you'd had a better day in London than I'd had here,' Jo went on, 'and he nearly bit my head off.'

Alandra made soothing noises that it appeared that Matt, for once, had not handled Jo with kid gloves, and that her cousin seemed more upset by that, than by any jealousy that he was out with Corinne Hamilton.

'Perhaps he needs a holiday,' said Jo thoughtfully, as she looked for excuses for him. 'He works so hard, yet he only ever takes a fortnight off each year. And I've never known him take any extra time off—well, except for that one day years ago when Grandfather was ill.'

Alandra had been content to let her talk the way Matt had been to her out of her system. But at the indication that her grandfather who looked never to have had a thing wrong with him, had been ill, she couldn't stop the, 'Grandfather was ill!' that left her.

'Oh, it was nothing serious,' Jo quickly discounted. 'And it was ages ago. I was only about fourteen at the time, but I remember Matt telling me to be specially nice to Grandfather because he'd had some bad news, and wasn't well.'

Alandra was silent for several moments. At fourteen, the same age as her cousin, her father had died and her mother had written to tell her grandfather about it. Was that the bad news which Matt had referred to? If so, it was more proof if she needed it—the fact that the news seemed to have laid her grandfather low—that he had indeed loved her father.

'What—er—exactly was wrong with him?' she asked, the need unexpectedly with her to get over an emotional moment.

'I don't quite know,' Jo replied. 'Some suggestion of a heart attack, I think. Anyhow, Matt had the doctor here quicker than that, and he didn't go to work all that day.'

Their grandfather and Robbie coming in at that point, took the talk back to her being in London, and how she had enjoyed her day.

Alandra left telling her grandfather of her decision to leave until Sunday. She had seen nothing of Matt since he had sped off for his date with Corinne Hamilton, and didn't know whether to be glad or sorry about that. He wasn't in to dinner on Sunday either.

Jealousy was tearing her apart when after dinner, having given her grandfather a few minutes to get his pipe alight, she went to his sitting room and knocked on the door.

'Come in,' he invited, puffing euphorically away at his pipe when she poked her head round the door. 'I don't bite.'

'I've had my anti-rabies jabs anyway,' she roused herself, and went in.

There wasn't a joke or a quip in her, though, when a minute later, ensconced in the easy chair opposite him, she saw that he wasn't looking too pleased with what she had just told him.

'You're leaving! Tomorrow!' he said. And shortly, 'What brought this on?'

'I didn't intend to stay so much as one night when I first came here,' she reminded him, her emotions out of gear again that by the sound of it, he did not want her to go.

'Going to London has unsettled you,' he pronounced. 'You were quite content here before you took yourself off on Friday.'

'I . . .' she said, and couldn't remember then when last she had been content, because she certainly wasn't now. 'I need to work, Grandfather,' she said as gently as she could. 'I've—had a good rest. In fact, quite a holiday,' she smiled. 'But, I need my independence,' and again she told him, 'I need to work.'

'Well that's no problem,' he came back, nodding at her need for independence. Only to have her jumping in rapidly, when he added, 'Matt will soon find you a secretarial job down at the plant.'

'No!' She looked away from his shrewd eyes at her instant and sharp refusal of such a suggestion. 'I couldn't . . .' she said lamely, and hoped he had missed how the thought of working for Matt had her horrified, yet at the same time longing to do just that.

He had caught the horrified bit, she knew that, when after a few seconds of silence, he quietly remarked, 'I thought you enjoyed slugging it out with Matt?'

'You've noticed,' she said, forcing a grin, which on the face of it, was all that she could do.

'Ah,' he said, which terrified her for a minute that he had read her secret. But only to have her relaxing when he revealed that he had witnessed something else, something that had nothing at all to do with Matt. 'It isn't Matt, is it? It's Robert.' She could almost see his brain ticking over, as he brought out, 'You know he's infatuated with you, of course?'

She nodded, starting to breathe easily. 'He'll soon get over it,' she said.

'But not while you're around, is that it? Is that why you don't want to work at the plant—because you know that Robert will want to take you there every day, and bring you home in the evening?'

It would have been so easy to latch on to that as an excuse for leaving, for not wanting to go and work at the offices of Carstairs and Todd. Her grandfather, although he seldom showed his affection, loved Robbie, she was convinced of that, and would, she thought, agree that it would be best if she left and so let Robbie get over his infatuation. But, in her view, it was less than honest to let Robbie be the scapegoat.

'I shan't be far away,' was the answer she gave him. And saw, unable to do better, that he was going to believe what he wanted to believe anyway, even though she had side-tracked him for a change, as he shelved any further questions on that score, and asked:

'You'll keep in touch? You don't intend to disappear out of our lives now that we've found you?'

'What sort of a girl do you think I am!' she asked smiling.

'A rather lovely one,' he said. And seemed then to have shocked himself as much as her on being so open with his praise. For he was then grunting, 'You're going to say "No" I suppose if I offer to make you the same quarterly allowance I make Josephine?'

Matt had intimated that her grandfather was no longer wealthy, but his offer of an allowance showed her that there was a very wide gap between her idea of being hard up and theirs.

'It's not your money I object to, Grandfather,' she answered, and that seemed to please him, even as he recognised that she could not accept. 'But . . .'

'I know,' he said, 'you like to be independent.'

Alandra smiled at his understanding. And she had only one last thing to say before she left him to smoke his pipe in peace.

'Can you—can you not tell anybody that I'm going until after I've gone?'

Sternly he looked at her. She knew his mind had gone to Robbie, but her mind was on Matt. She was sure Matt would speed her on her way with something vitriolic that she was going back on her word to stay three months, and she didn't want that. Even while for pride's sake she didn't mind him thinking that she so loved the man she had gone to London to meet that day, that she was prepared to forfeit the thousand pounds he had offered just so she could spend more time with him, she just did not want to part from Matt with the sour taste of his acid remarks in her ears.

'You have my word on it,' said her grandfather after a lengthy silence. 'I shall tell no one of your plans, Alandra, until you are safely away.'

The following morning she went down to breakfast, and knew that if she had arrived at Roseacres with hate in her heart, then she was leaving with only love there for each of its inhabitants.

Only her grandfather and Matt were down as yet. But as she took her seat, so her eyes rested on the charcoal-grey suited man who held more of her heart than any of them.

Oh, how she loved him, she thought, and had to quickly avert her eyes from the hard ice she saw Matt's eyes held for her, as without warning just then, he looked across at her.

Not daring to look at him again for fear her eyes

would give her away, she heard his abrupt movement.
And the next she knew was that Matt, without a word
to either her or her grandfather, had left the table, had
left the room.

And she knew then that she need not have worried
about his last words to her being of the acid variety—
for she had said goodbye to him, without one word
having been spoken.

Alandra gazed unseeing over the top of her typewriter,
and wondered yet again when the pain of leaving
Roseacres would begin to ease. Over the last seven
weeks she had grown thinner, and she knew that
Hector, for all he had said nothing, had noticed a
change in her. She guessed that he was putting the times
she would come to and find she had been staring into
space, down to the fact that she was still upset over her
mother's death. And she did not disabuse him. She still
thought often of her mother, but much more often, it
was Matt Carstairs who filled her mind. And she just
seemed incapable of ejecting him. He was her constant
companion, and the ache in her heart never looked like
healing.

That first month back in her flat had been terrible,
she recalled, not dwelling on the fact that this second
month had not been any easier. But going back over
that first month when first one week had gone by, and
then another had dragged to a close, Alandra
remembered the end of the third week when it had
taken every morsel of self-control not to give in and
take a train to Ferny Druffield.

She had felt stronger at the beginning of the fourth
week, but by the time Friday had come around, she had
again been very much tempted. Just to see Matt would
have been enough, she thought, and had fought a
mighty battle not to give in.

Though in the end, prompted by memory of the
promise to her grandfather to keep in touch, and telling

herself she was only keeping a promise and that it was not weakness on her part, she had telephoned Roseacres.

Matt's voice was the one she wanted to hear, but it was at a time when she knew he would be at his office that she rang her grandfather. He had sounded pleased to hear her, and not a bit grumpy, she recalled, as he had asked how she was and told her that they were all missing her.

'Even Matt?' She hadn't been able to resist the question.

'Something's not going right for him at any rate,' her grandfather had replied, and her ridiculous heart knew a joyous upsurge that Matt might be out of sorts because she was not there! Truly ridiculous, she thought, and then that idea was knocked on the head when he followed up with, 'Josephine reckons he's in love, and that Corinne Hamilton is giving him a tough time.'

'Er—How is Jo?' she asked quickly, covering madly the effect his words were having on her.

'She, like Matt, has taken to preferring to dine elsewhere,' he answered with a touch of humour.

'Jonathan Naseby?' she guessed, gathering from that that whether or not Corinne Hamilton was giving Matt a tough time, he was still constantly taking her out to dinner. And heard her grandfather confirm that Jonathan Naseby's car was often seen on the drive at Roseacres these days, to which he added:

'Thank God she seems finally to be getting over her crush for Matt.' And straight away afterwards, 'Are you coming home for my birthday next month? I'll be seventy on the sixteenth.'

That word, so naturally brought out, 'home' had her eyes moist. 'You're having a party?' she asked, and excitement began immediately to stir that seventy was a special birthday, and she had a tailor-made excuse to visit Roseacres. But that was before visions of all the family being there, Jo with Jonathan Naseby, Matt with ... And she knew then as excitement died, that she would not be setting a foot near.

Her grandfather exclaiming, 'Party! Who do you think would come?' had her quickly collecting herself.

'You're not that *bad*,' she answered. And invented hurriedly, 'Though trust you to choose to have a birthday on the one and only day I've made other arrangements I can't get out of.'

Alandra put the phone down having promised she would ring him on his seventieth birthday, but her mind more taken up with the knowledge that if he was not having a party as such, then without doubt Matt would arrange some sort of dinner celebration where Corinne Hamilton was sure to be invited.

Hector coming in through the office door had her realising that she had gone off again in the middle of her typing.

The Monday before her grandfather's birthday on the Thursday, she parcelled up the cardigan she had bought him, together with the matching skein of darning wool—it might make him smile even if he preferred to wear his old much-darned one.

There was a longing with her on Tuesday when she mailed her parcel, to take it to Roseacres personally. That same longing was there with her on Wednesday as she stood at the post-box with the birthday card addressed to her grandfather. Visions of Corinne Hamilton probably sitting in her chair at the dining table—or, more likely, sitting next to Matt—had her posting the card and hurrying away.

Thursdays at the office were usually quiet. But because she had intended to make her promised call to her grandfather first thing, that morning turned out to be the sort where she needed three pairs of hands at once.

Things calmed down during the afternoon, but wanting to make her call at a time when Matt would not be there, it was four o'clock before she had the chance. And her hand was actually on the phone when Hector chose to remind her of a call he was expecting, and asked her would she mind fetching him a cheese roll from Mario's.

'I'd go myself,' he explained, as she got to her feet, 'but that call's bound to come in the moment I go through the door, and—I'm starving.'

'You'll get fat,' she told him, but she was already on her way.

With time going on and partly because she didn't want to tie up the office phone if Hector's call hadn't come through when she got back, Alandra decided as she neared the telephone kiosk that stood a hundred yards up the street from Mario's sandwich bar, that she would make use of it.

It was in her mind as she dialled to trill off with a bright rendering of 'Happy birthday to you'. But as the phone was picked up straight away, and a voice that wasn't her grandfather's came across the wires in the short space before the rapid pips went, everything instantly went out of her head. That was Matt!

With no recollection of having dropped the receiver back on its rest, or of moving, Alandra found she was outside the kiosk. And it was only when a passer-by looked at her strangely that she gathered her scattered senses together, and started to walk towards Mario's.

The cheese roll secure in a paper bag in her hands, she moved from the counter, the thought still rattling round in her head—what was Matt doing at home at this time of the day?

Perhaps he had come home early because of grandfather's birthday? But did that fit? Her grandfather wasn't having a party so he had said, and if there was to be a dinner party, then Mrs Pinder could cope very nicely on her own.

She was nearing the phone box again, when the memory hit her of Jo telling her once that Matt never

had any time off from work other than the two weeks'
holiday he allowed himself—that was, except for that
day when her grandfather had been ill with a suspected
heart attack!

Panic hit her. And confusion. So that she was inside
the telephone booth not at all sure that it had been
Matt's voice she had heard in the brief space of time
between the connection and the pips.

Emotion only motivating her, she was soon dialling
the same number she had not many minutes before
dialled. Realisation with her then of how much she had
come to love her grandfather.

There was no voice in her ear this time when the
phone at Roseacres was picked up. And, when she had
put her money in and the pips had stopped, there was
still no voice at the other end to tell her who had
answered. She saw then that whoever it was must be
waiting for her to speak first.

'H-hello,' she stammered, and in the pause that
followed, she was suddenly beset by nerves.

Her nerves were in no way quietened when, after
what seemed an age, her shaky 'Hello' was answered.
Because it was Matt's voice that came back to her, his
tone sounding strange—controlled—and, was there a
touch of tension there? She was tense herself, and was
gripping hard on to the phone as from that 'Hello' Matt
had obviously recognised her voice.

'Don't hang up again, Alandra,' he told her, having her
knowing that it *had* been Matt who had answered before.

'Grandfather . . .?' she said, her fears for her
grandparent getting her over the weakness that just
hearing Matt aroused.

'You're needed here,' he replied, all the answer there
she required for her to know that her grandfather must
be desperately ill.

She swallowed hard. 'Is he . . .?' she asked fearfully.
And heard just how urgent it was when Matt replied,
his voice carefully even now:

'Tell me where you live, Alandra. I'll come . . .'

Tears were in her eyes when she left the telephone box. What—Matt had said after that 'I'll come . . .' or if indeed he had uttered anything, she couldn't have said. Because the fact that he had intimated he would come and collect her must mean that there was not much time, that it would be quicker in his fast car for him to collect her than for her to hang about waiting for a train.

But Matt loved her grandfather as much as she did. He would not want to leave his side, not now. Nor was it right that, because of her, he should do so.

'You're needed here,' he had said. And that could only mean, she thought, as struggling for control she pushed her way into the office, that her grandfather was asking for her.

'That call came through . . .' Hector began. Then he looked up and saw how white-faced she was. 'What on earth's happened?' he asked. And was already coming to help her into a seat, as haltingly Alandra told him how she had just telephoned her grandfather's home and learned how very ill he was.

'I'm going to him,' she stated, too fidgety to sit, getting up from her chair. 'I'll ring the station and . . .'

'You're going nowhere by train the state you're in,' said her kindly boss straight away. 'I'll drive you.'

And taking complete charge because he could see that she was too upset to be thinking in any ordered pattern, he then suggested that 'things' might not be as bad as she anticipated, but that it could be she might have to stay a few days. He went on to suggest that she go up to her flat and throw a few things into a case while he cleared up and telephoned Bianca to tell her he would be a little late.

'You don't mind?' she thought to ask. 'Bianca won't mind?'

He smiled encouragingly, not her employer any more, but her friend. 'Don't worry, love,' he said, going to the door with her, 'I'll soon have you delivered to your family.' And revealing he had witnessed her many times when she had been unaware of it, 'I don't think in your heart you ever left them, did you?'

Alandra looked at him, comforted by the calm way he was organising everything. And there was not a scrap of evasion or an impulse to lie in her then, as honestly, she replied:

'No, I never did.'

CHAPTER TEN

HER thoughts on that journey from London were anguished and of nightmare proportions. But when Hector drew the car to a halt on the drive of Roseacres, Alandra thought the least she could do, fearful as she was of what she might find inside, was to invite him in for some sort of refreshment before he started his return journey.

But, having overcome his surprise that her family seemed to be very well set up, if the large imposing residence he had brought her to was anything to go by, Hector recovered sufficiently to give her hand a squeeze, and tell her:

'I don't think so, in the circumstances, thanks, love.' And handing over the small case she had packed, he said, 'Bianca will be waiting. Don't hesitate to ring home or the office if we can be of assistance.' And when she thanked him sincerely, he smiled and instructed her, 'Be brave, be plucky, Alandra—like you always are.'

He had driven away by the time she had mounted the steps and was standing waiting for her ring at the bell to be answered. 'Be brave,' he had said, but she wasn't feeling brave. She knew she would need all her reserves of strength not to break down and cry if things were as bad with her grandfather as she thought they must be from Matt's tense, 'You're needed here.'

Footsteps coming along the hall, someone on the other side of the door, had her straightening her shoulders and swallowing hard on her fear.

Oddly, she had thought that Matt or one of the others would have opened the door. But she was quickly to wonder what she was thinking of when Mrs Pinder, a surprised to see her Mrs Pinder, stood back from the door and beamed a smile at her. Of course, Matt, Jo and Robbie would be grouped around her grandfather's bed, she thought, stepping over the threshold. But there was some surprise about Alandra, too. Mrs Pinder, although she had always got on well with her, was not looking as sad as she would have expected. She wasn't family, but she had worked for . . .

'My grandfather . . .' she said, her voice quiet and as controlled as she could make it. Realisation with her that she was wasting time standing there analysing why the housekeeper should be looking so cheerful to see her.

'He'll be so pleased to see you,' Mrs Pinder replied.

Alandra stared at her solemnly, then looked to the stairs. 'I'll go up to him,' she said. And she had moved off a couple of paces before what the housekeeper said registered. 'What did you say?' she enquired turning.

'He's not in his room upstairs,' was repeated. And Alandra knew sick foreboding that she had arrived too late. Then Mrs Pinder was adding, 'He's in his sitting room.'

Alandra moved rapidly then, her case dropping from her hand as she raced to the sitting room, fear with her that if she had not arrived too late, then her grandfather must be too ill to be moved.

She entered the sitting room without knocking, and it was just as she had remembered it. There was the same three-piece, the same cosy fire, the same pale grey carpet. But there was no sign of a hastily installed bed—and no sign at all of Matt or her two cousins!

But it was when a movement at the small desk over by the window had her eyes shooting over to it that she experienced a shock so great that for some seconds the power of speech was taken away from her.

For slowly, the man she had dashed to see, the man she thought needed her there, started to rise from the wooden-backed chair he was seated in. And as Alandra watched in stunned silence, gradually, the broadest smile she had ever seen on him began to break over her grandfather's face. And while she was able to take in that there was a joy in him to see her there on his birthday, she was also able to see—that there was nothing whatsoever the matter with him!

'Alandra!' he exclaimed, his pleasure obvious. 'You came after all!'

'Gr-grand—father,' she stammered, moving forward from where she had stood rooted, the words 'You're needed here. Tell me where you live. I'll come . . .' spinning around in her head.

'You promised you would ring,' he said, smiling still as he too came forward and met her in the middle of the room. 'I was beginning to think it had slipped your mind.'

Getting over her shock, she took one of the two easy chairs he indicated, and seated herself opposite him while it sank in that Matt had not yet told him that she had already made her promised call to Roseacres.

'You are—you're well, Grandfather?' she asked, doubt coming about his look of health on remembering that there had been days when her mother had looked well, when that was very far from being the case.

'I'm much better for seeing you,' he owned with a smile.

He *is* ill, she thought, and gently she asked, 'Has the doctor been to see you?'

'Doctor?' His smile had gone as with a touch of his old asperity, he replied, 'Just because I'm seventy, it doesn't mean I'm decrepit.' And confirming for her that Matt, for some reason she didn't have time to go into just then, had pulled a fast one on her, he was adding, 'I haven't seen a doctor since the day . . .' he paused and amended, 'since some years ago when Matt took it into his head to decide I should be checked over.'

Anger that had begun to spiral in her against Matt, cooled slightly at the memory of just why her grandfather had needed to have a doctor attend him 'some years ago'. Though it was to take quite a struggle

before she was able to bite down on all her anger
against Matt, and find a smile as she told her
grandfather:

'Just checking.' And impishly, 'Your smile rather
threw me when I came in . . .' She didn't have to finish.

'You thought I must be sickening for something to
give you such a spontaneous smile?' he finished for her.
And she actually heard a chuckle break from him.

Then she was back to thinking of Matt—he never
was far away from her. And anger was in her again, for
all she kept a smile on her face, as she said:

'Actually this is only a flying visit.' And making it up
as she went along. 'A friend of mine has an errand in
this part of the world and is waiting outside to get on. I
said I'd only be two minutes.'

'Seems a long way to come for only two minutes,' he
replied, letting her know it hadn't taken long for the
chuckle to disappear and the grumpy man she knew
better to come to the fore.

'Not if a girl wants to wish a personal "Happy
birthday" to a grandparent she had been determined to
hate,' she began to tease, but her tone going serious on
her, as truthfully she found herself ending, 'but has
discovered that she does not.'

The grouch in him disappeared, as quietly, he asked,
'You're—fond of me, child?'

Tears wanted to come to the surface. 'In spite of
myself,' she nodded.

And found then, that touched by her confession as the
moisture in his eyes proved, he was still every bit of the
wily old fox she had very early on learned that he was.

'In that case why not send your chauffeur away?' he
was quick to suggest. 'Matt's gone out somewhere at
the moment, but he has organised a bit of a dinner
party despite my protests.' She was already backing
away from the idea before he had finished speaking.
'Josephine's young man will be here, and even Robert is
bringing a girl he met in . . .'

'I can't, Grandfather,' she jumped in quickly.

Her agitation had her on her feet, her mind soon having worked out that Matt must have gone to pick up Corinne. She couldn't, just couldn't, be around when the pair of them got back. Even furious with him as she was for the way he had tricked her, she just could not face him bringing Corinne Hamilton over the threshold of Roseacres.

'I told you this was only a flying visit, you know I have other arrangements for this evening,' she rushed on, when not pleased to have his idea thwarted, her grandfather frowned heavily at her. 'Forgive me,' she said simply then. And when he didn't look very forgiving, she did what she wanted to do, she bent and kissed his leathery old cheek.

His frown had gone when she straightened up, she saw, something near a smile hovering when, gruffly, he said, 'Be off with you, then.' But he did have a smile for her, when at the door she turned, 'And make sure you ring me soon so that I can thank you properly for my new cardigan,' he added, and smiled.

Alandra closed the door quietly behind her, no idea in her head of how she was going to get back to London. She closed her eyes and leaned against the door needing a few moments to marshal her thoughts into constructive thinking.

Then, as a sense of urgency came, the thought taking precedence that it didn't matter how she got back to London, but that she had to get out of the house before it was too late, abruptly, she opened her eyes.

Her body had been ready for flight. But as her lids opened, and her eyes widened, so her limbs just refused to obey the instructions they were receiving from her brain.

For as she stared mortified across the wide hall to the front door, so her feet felt concreted to the ground. And the sight of Matt, not yet changed for dinner, dressed in navy trousers and a sweater, was all that was needed to tell her she had delayed her departure too long—that she had left it too late!

That he was alone did not for the moment register as she stood and stared at him. He looked thinner, she thought, her heart setting up a calamitous thudding.

A movement to the left of her had her dragging her eyes from him, and going to see the housekeeper who was just about to disappear from view at the top of the stairs. But that was not all—she had disappeared with her case!

And never more glad was Alandra then, than to feel that spurt of anger that came and freed her from her frozen immobility.

'What's Mrs Pinder doing with my case!' she flashed by way of a greeting, already on her way to charge up the stairs in pursuit of it.

Matt too had moved, not making her anger diminish by the cool way he met her at the bottom of the stairs and informed her as he barred her access:

'I told her to take it to your room.'

'Well you can just jolly well order her to bring it down again,' she said heatedly, her efforts to go racing up the stairs blocked, 'I'm leaving—*now*,' she underlined. Though she made no attempt to push past him. Matt was looking to be in one of his determined moods, and she didn't want his hands on her if he chose not to let her pass.

'How did you get here?' he asked, ignoring her bossing him about, as if she had not spoken. Well, she could do some ignoring too, she thought, having no intention of answering him. But that was before he caught at the perversity in her by stating, just as though he knew it for a fact, 'You didn't come by train.'

'How do you know I didn't?' she asked belligerently.

'I've just been to meet the London train—you weren't on it,' he replied.

Which skittled her, she had to admit. Pleased her too, though she would have liked to deny it, that it was not to pick up Corinne Hamilton that he had gone out, but by the sound of it, had gone to the railway station on the off chance she might have managed to be on the train from London.

'Well—I hope you caught pneumonia while waiting,' was the poor best she could come up with. And for her trouble had his eyes going over her as he took in her physical condition.

'You've lost weight—you're thinner,' he said frowning.

'Aren't we all,' she replied snappily.

An alert look came to him then, and she had to suffer his steady thoughtful gaze for long drawn out moments before, softly, slowly at last, he asked:

'For the same reason, Alandra, I wonder?'

She knew then, that with or without her case, it was time she went. Without a doubt, jealousy stabbing, she knew that Matt had lost his appetite through the tough time Corinne Hamilton was giving him and the love he felt for her. But with his 'For the same reason?' fresh in her ears, Alandra felt she would just die if he discerned that it was her hopeless love for him that was making all food taste like chaff in her mouth.

About to leave without her case, at just that moment Mrs Pinder came to the top of the stairs and began to descend. When Matt stepped to one side and Mrs Pinder passed by, Alandra did not waste a second.

Racing up the stairs, she had made it to the door of her old room before it dawned on her what an idiot she was. Matt was right there with her. Though, since it seemed he had not finished with her yet, he could equally well have followed her outside, she realised, had she bolted for the outside door.

That he still had business with her was made plain when, before her hand could reach to open her door, he had caught hold of her, and had turned her to face him. And just as she had known it would, to have his hands touching her had the most dreadful weakening effect, so that she was having to fight with all she had to beat it.

'Take your hands off me,' she hissed. And found that he still wasn't interested in being bossed about by her, as her request was denied. 'I object to being manhandled by a liar,' she fumed, having a second try. Only to be made infuriated when not letting go of her, calmly, he replied:

'When have I ever lied to you?'

'When?'

Flabbergasted that he could ask such a thing, she stared in astonishment. He was just too much, and there was no holding back on her temper as rage in her erupted, and she let fly:

'Why the hell do you think I'm here if it's not because you said it was important that I get here quickly?'

It wasn't quite what he had said, but it amounted to the same thing. She was too het up then anyway to remember his exact words.

But Matt she saw wasn't going in for nit-picking, as looking her calmly straight in the eye, he set her rage blistering as he said:

'I was not lying.'

'You were!' she exploded. 'You know you were.' And not letting him cut in, 'I've just seen my grandfather—there's nothing at all the matter with him.' She gave another ineffectual pull to get out of his hold, and her rocketing temper received another booster that still he wasn't letting her go. 'You deceived me!' she yelled, 'You deceived me into thinking . . .'

'Just as you have deceived me and *my* thinking many times,' he stated, his voice cool and controlled in stark contrast to her utter fury. 'Many times you have deliberately led me up false trails,' he accused. And heat coming, 'Deliberately, you set me up to think you were a money-chasing hard case.'

For long seconds she made no move to struggle out of the grip he now had on both of her arms. And it was wordlessly that she stared at him, never more shaken to realise, if she had got it right, that Matt must now be saying that he no longer believed that she had come to Roseacres because she had been after all she could get!

Memory of the thousand pounds she had spurned hit her, and she was struggling again to be free, the jibing words coming, 'Don't tell me you've changed your opinion *just* because I left without asking for part of that thousand you promised.'

Her reference to the money had rattled him, she could see that—and feel it—as he shook her to be still, then rapped impatiently:

'Oh, for God's sake! I'd rumbled you before you left.' And as if the knowledge that he had ever offered her money was distasteful to him, he pulled her with him to the door opposite from the door she wanted to go through.

A second later she found herself in that part of the house in which she had never before trespassed. And with his eyes intent on her as he closed the door of his private apartment, she began to suspect that the only reason she had been allowed to gallop up those stairs in the first place, was so that he could get her into his private sitting room where they could not be overheard or interrupted. Though why, she could not guess!

But by then she was not thinking very clearly, instinct her only companion; that instinct was telling her she had better get out of there with all speed! But although Matt had let go of her, he was standing between her and the door, and he had that determined light in his eyes again.

'If you've brought me in here so you can fling some more of your vile insults at me, then you have another think coming. You can just open that door and let me out again,' she said, nervous of him, and knowing she was right to be nervous of him.

He had witnessed her nervousness, she was aware of that, because she made no move to go anywhere near him, or make any attempt to push him aside. And he was as receptive to her orders as he had ever been, too, she saw. Then he did move, and it was towards her—and the door was still behind him.

'I've said some terrible things to you, and I know it,' he said. 'The worst of all, I suspect, in frightening you half to death about your grandfather—though, although you won't believe it, it wasn't until after you'd put the phone down on me that I came to realise—loving Alain as you do—that from the few words I said your lively imagination would have him at death's door.'

'You believe I—love him?'

She had not meant to ask that question. It was the shock that had loosened her tongue, she supposed. Shock, because, believing nothing good about her, Matt, without her having to say so, appeared to know that she had grown to love the man who had disowned her father.

'Of course,' he replied. And would have added more, only she was suddenly sensing a weakening in her defences, and was rushing in there to hurriedly repair them.

'I didn't mean to . . .' she stopped, then went quickly on again. 'I hated him at first,' she said. 'I—I was determined to hate him for ever more.'

Matt's smile was quizzical, as if he knew that too, even if he didn't understand why. 'But you couldn't keep it up,' he stated.

She frowned. 'I would have done had I left that first Saturday,' she said firmly, trying for a coldness that wasn't there. 'Only—only, well—everything sort of ganged up against me.' She shrugged expressively, as she listed, 'Lack of trains, Jo and Robbie being thorough snobs—as I thought then. And you . . .' She halted again as she began to wonder how she had got started on this conversation?

'And with me accepting the front you were showing, without so much as bothering to look beneath the surface of you, you decided to take me up on my offer to pay you to stay, for the pure pleasure it would give you to tell me what I could do with my cheque when I handed it over,' he said. Throwing her again, because if by his own admission he had not bothered to look beneath the surface of her at the beginning, then, by the look of it, he had taken a very deep look beneath the surface since she had left.

And that, Alandra thought with a flutter of panic, had to mean that she was skating on very thin ice. Hastily she searched for, and by the skin of her teeth found, the combat weapon that had been such an ally to her in the past.

'Really, Matt dear,' she said loftily, not missing that his eyes had narrowed at the change in her attitude—her grandfather would call it saucy, she knew he would. 'You mustn't go around imagining like my grandfather, that I'm solely my father's daughter and want none of the material things in life.'

'You're suggesting you have a mercenary streak inherited from your mother?' he queried, his face expressionless, and she would dearly have loved to have known what he was thinking.

She had expected him to fire a salvo back at her as in the past he had not hesitated to do. And she was thrown again that he did not. So that even though she wanted hotly to repudiate that her mother had any streak in her at all that wasn't giving and kind, she held down hard on the impulse, and was lofty again, as airily, she told him:

'Grandfather found it necessary to reply to her letter acquainting him with my father's death, to the effect that if it was her intention to write again asking for a handout, then she could save herself a stamp—work it out for yourself,' she added carelessly.

But she was to wish that she had not. For it seemed Matt was more than halfway there to working it out without the need of any invitation from her. And his eyes had narrowed again, when sharply, he threw at her:

'This letter from Alain to your mother—when did you first see it?'

'I never poked through my mother's personal belongings when she was alive, if that's what you're hinting,' she snapped. But she had to know then when his face cleared that another piece of the puzzle she had made of herself had just fallen into place. There was even a trace of a smile on his mouth, when softly, he said:

'So that's it!'

She shrugged, when she had never felt less like shrugging, and she was never more wary of him. Matt was still guarding the way out; even if he was closer to her than he was to the door.

'That's what?' she felt compelled to ask, even if she did manage to make her voice sound as though she was not particularly interested in his answer.

His smile was still about him as quietly he said, 'That was the reason you came here ready to hate Alain— your mother had just died, and you had found a letter from him that must have caused her pain.' Alandra blinked dry-mouthed as, accurately, he went on. 'That was the reason why, had the railway timetable not been against you, had I not pricked your Todd pride by daring to offer you money, you would not have deigned to spend a moment longer at Roseacres than it took for you to hand that letter back to Alain.'

'My mother asked me to come,' she quickly inserted.

With Matt slotting all the pieces neatly into place, she was panicking again, and trying to side-track him, for soon he would have it all. Soon he would be knowing why it was she had bolted—and she couldn't have that.

'When she was dying?'

Her astounded gasp at his sharp guesswork was all the confirmation he needed. For he paused only briefly, before going on.

'Obviously your mother asked you to come to Roseacres because she loved you, and could not bear to think of you all alone in the world when you had a family not too far away.'

Matt stating what had come to her as the truth in the many weeks she had had to think about it, his reminding her of how much her mother must have loved her to have made that request, did nothing to give her the stiffening she needed.

'You're forgetting,' she said, trying to overcome emotion, 'that I—I have done very nicely out of my—my extended stay here.' And having to go on when he raised a querying eyebrow as though he couldn't see how, since she had refused the car her grandfather had offered her. 'Those—pearls, are really magnificent.'

He smiled, and she was wary again. And was right to be wary, she saw, when smoothly, he dropped out, 'I'll agree, they are magnificent. Surprising too how much they have increased in value since last they were valued for insurance purposes.' It was her turn to look questioning, though not for very long as he went on just as smoothly to advise, 'It was only last week that Alain asked me to take them to be re-assessed—and it was by the way that he mentioned that he wasn't too happy to tell me you had refused to accept the offer of your grandmother's pearls, Alandra.'

Floundering, she plucked out another memory, 'And you weren't too happy either, were you, dear Matt, when you saw me coming from Grandfather's sitting room with a handful of notes that day I went to London?'

Thinking that she had at last got him off the track his mind, now of all times, had seemed set on, seeking to discover the real her, she was left gaping when he said:

'Have you forgotten that the night before I had held you, moist-eyed, in my arms? There was no pretence about you then.'

'How—do you know?' she challenged, and knew she was struggling.

'Because it was then, like I said,' he answered coolly, 'that I rumbled you, Alandra.'

'Oh,' she said, and was then having to backtrack quickly on how this change in the conversation had come about. 'Yes, well,' she murmured, and was again challenging, 'You were as mad as hell at breakfast about the money I had wheedled out of my grandfather.'

'Wheedled?' he questioned, his face creasing. 'If I know Alain, he's foxy enough to have had you taking that money whether you wanted to or not.'

And while she was chewing on that, and the thought that if Matt hadn't been mad because of the money, then what the heck' had he been mad about at breakfast? because furious he certainly had been, smoothly, he was letting fall:

'Did I mention, by the way, that he told me you were too proud, too independent, to accept the offer of the allowance he would have liked to have made you?'

Alandra knew then that he had her cold. And unable to do anything else, she had to admit defeat. 'So, okay,' she said, having run out of ammunition, her cover blown, her one desire now to leave before he did any more analysing, 'I'll admit I'm all the lovely things you never believed until that night ...' she broke off on finding herself still in choppy waters. 'If you'll excuse me,' she amended politely, 'I'll say goodni ...'

Matt's hand on her arm caught her as she would have passed him. He swung her round to face him, even as she was holding down on the words to plead with him to let her go. She could not afford to show him how much just being in the same room with him weakened her. Or just how much the feel of his hand on her arm made her want to crumple against him.

Striving hard for every ounce of backbone, she did what she could in the way of mustering all the disdain she could manage to look haughtily down at the hand on her arm.

But his short bark of laughter, his, 'Oh God, Alandra, you're priceless,' quickly had her phoney disdain evaporating.

'Now what did I do?' she questioned.

His laughter had gone, and she was further undermined to hear him say softly, 'We came in here for some privacy so you could slam into me for scaring you so badly about Alain's health,' just as though she had voluntarily entered his apartment, she thought, starting to grow confused. 'We got diverted, I admit, though I'm hoping none of what we've said will be wasted,' he added, which didn't help in any way to clear the confusion she was wading ankle-deep in. 'But yet,' he went on, 'after all that—you are ready to *go* without endeavouring to bury a verbal hatchet in my head?'

Her mind darting all over the place, she searched around for excuses. 'You—confused me,' she felt forced to own, his dark eyes pinning hers, preventing all excuses for wanting to leave without first punching him on the nose, from presenting themselves.

'I'm sorry.' His voice was suddenly gentle, and this didn't help to clear her confusion.

'Well—er—don't do it again,' she said, and all of a sudden, she had to laugh.

But just as suddenly, she was no longer laughing. For he was looking at her, hearing her light amused laugh, and he was bending near and looking for all the world as though he would very much like to kiss her.

Quickly Alandra pulled her face out of range, her heart beating a wild rhythm she gave up trying to still as his mouth quirked and he muttered something about, 'having to go the long way round' which made no sense at all. Then she found he was taking her over to a settee in the room, and was making her sit there with him.

'I don't . . .' she said, and would have stood up—only Matt was saying:

'Don't you want to know why I found it necessary to tell you how desperately you are needed here?'

'Desperately?' she echoed, something—something she had never seen in his face before keeping her seated. There was a deadly serious look there, and ... and something else she couldn't quite define, purely, she thought, because she had never seen him looking that way before—at her, or anyone else.

'Yes, desperate,' he nodded. 'I know now, that you have been wanted here ever since that first day I saw you, sitting there in the drawing room with the sunlight making a golden halo of your hair.'

Her breathing felt choky. Matt had never looked, or spoken this way to her before. And she had to be glad that she was seated, for her legs were beginning to feel made of water. She fought hard to find a careless note, but it didn't quite come off, as with an attempt at lightness, she said:

'You've—missed me?' And realising that was much too pointed, as if it mattered to her that he alone might have missed her, 'All of you?' she added.

'All of us,' he confirmed. But it did nothing for her breathing that had about half a second to regularise itself, when he took hold of one of her hands lying on her lap, and said, 'But I have missed you more than anyone, Alandra.'

'Oh!' It was all she was capable of saying, as swallowing hard, she stared at him.

'You've been away too long,' he said, and had her striving hard not to melt as he raised the hand he held to his lips and kissed the back of it. 'That is why it was so important you returned with all haste. That was why I wasn't thinking straight, not thinking at all that you might panic over Alain,' he told her, adding, deliberately, '*I* needed you here.'

A trembling had made itself felt in her. She knew it had communicated itself to him, but whatever he was reading from her sudden trembling at the possessive '*I*' needed you here, she was powerless to stop the quivering, as, her voice gone husky, she asked:

'W-why?'

Gently he took hold of her other trembling hand. And gently, he kissed that hand too. 'Because I've been in hell ever since you went away,' he confessed, dragging from her, her own confession of a choky:

'I had—to go.'

The magnetism of him had her eyes staying with his, even though a warm pink colour had started to invade her cheeks. A voice in her head wanted to be heard, that voice that said she should be running, now, while she still had her pride intact. But he was still holding on to her hands, and, she very much doubted, even if she felt like obeying the voice in her head, that her legs would have held her.

'I hope I know why you felt you had to go,' Matt said softly, which had her flushing again, but still unable to look away from him, as he went on quietly. 'Though at first I couldn't believe you had gone. And then I was furious with you that you had. And then furious with myself that it should matter to me.'

Alandra's gasp was faint, but audible. And he leaned forward to gently kiss the side of her flushed face. And then, since nothing coherent was coming from her, he pulled back just when it looked as though he would possess her mouth with his, and continued:

'I had asked you to stay, telling myself that it was only for Alain's sake that I had asked you.'

'But—it—wasn't?' she dared with as much voice as she had.

He shook his head. 'I've only recently admitted to myself why,' he owned. 'I wouldn't admit it even when the house was dead without you there to stir the adrenalin with your lip—the morning starting off dully without your bright "Good morning". But when your parcel came for Alain, and it hit me that since you weren't delivering it in person—when you loved him and knew that three score and ten was a special birthday to him—I knew that never did you intend to set foot inside Roseacres again, and I had to admit it then.'

Her throat had gone dry, but she just had to force out the words, 'What—did you have to ...' she swallowed, '... admit, Matt?'

'You haven't guessed?'

She shook her head and desperately needed to be told. And she swallowed again, and coloured again, when tenderly his hand came to caress the side of her face.

'You haven't guessed that I've been going quietly out of my mind with thoughts of you in London with some man you once told me you were in love with?'

Involuntarily, her hands gripped on to his hand. And a half smile was there on his mouth for her, as he said:

'No, I'm sure you can have no idea of how it felt that I should live through days—weeks—of having the thought of you constantly with me. The thought that if you were just half the girl I had seen that night breaking her heart when she thought she had the kitchen to herself, and were not anything at all like the girl who was trying to make me believe couldn't care less what the hell I thought of her, then I could well have been instrumental in driving you away.'

Alandra knew fear and hope, and was gulping again, as she struggled for words, 'You—didn't want to dr-drive me away?' she asked. And she saw the answer there in his sincere dark eyes, as he smiled tenderly and said:

'I want you here, Alandra. Here in my home—permanently.' And never more tenderly, 'It is where you belong, my dear.'

Alandra sighed. But, she was still fearful she had got it wrong. And her trembling increased, as she had to ask, praying that she was wrong:

'Be-because I'm Alain Todd's granddaughter?'

Gently he took her by the shoulders. And deeply he looked into her wide green eyes. 'Because you hold my heart, my darling,' he whispered tenderly.

His whispered words, the 'my darling' he had breathed, had her hands gripping tightly together in her lap. Matt had to mean that he loved her, didn't he? In spite of the way, apart from that one time, they had done nothing but square up to each other—it had to mean that he loved her, didn't it? She remembered the exhilaration she had always felt after crossing swords with Matt. Had it been the same for him? Had love, in a roundabout way, been in the air then? There was so much she wanted to ask him. From the look of him, he was waiting for her to say something—but, she felt swamped by what he had said, and felt incapable then of uttering a sound. And he was beginning to look, for the first time since she had known him, to be strangely unsure.

'Am I so totally wrong to have thought it impossible for you to respond the way you do when you're in my arms, and yet be in love with someone else?' he asked, his voice having a gritty note to it, as his eyes searched her face. And when she was still too choked to say anything, he went on, tension showing in his face, 'Am I wrong to think you're nervous of me, that you were nervous of me when you saw me, that your trembling now is not because you feel something for me other than the hate I deserve from you?'

'Matt . . .' she cried in protest. But sorely wanting to tell him that no, that she did not hate him, her emotions were still choking her, and her voice was a croak, and his name was all that would come from her.

'Am I wrong,' he said, tension not limited to his face as his fingers dug hard into her shoulders, 'to think that those moments of empathy we shared that night I found you weeping, were special moments that could be stretched,' his jaw was working she saw, as he ended, 'and could be made permanent?'

She knew then from the agony of waiting in his eyes, that she had to surface from the emotions in her that were threatening to have tears of joy rolling down her cheeks. For Matt looked to be a man at the end of his tether—and she just could not bear to see him so uncertain.

'You're—you're saying—that you l-love me?' she managed to ask, an unsuspected shyness trapping her so that she could not answer any one of his questions.

'I'm saying,' Matt answered, hiding nothing, ready now to take it if his calculations had all been wide of the mark, 'that I adore you, Alandra.'

Tears did come to her eyes, and they were those joyful tears of encouragement, accompanied by a loving smile so that Matt told her:

'I love you so much my dear, dear Alandra, that I shall never know another moment's peace until you are my wife.'

The tears she had hoped to hold back could no longer be retained. First one soft globule welled over and fell, and then another, and at her breathy sigh of, 'Oh Matt!' he had pulled her into his arms. And it was utter bliss to her to be resting against him, his arms around her, as with infinite tenderness he gently kissed her brow.

Then still with her in his hold, he moved her slightly away so that he could look into her face. Gently he wiped away her tears, and it was for ageless moments that they just stared at each other. She saw some of the tension had gone from him as, her eyes gentle on him, there was no mistaking what was in her heart.

And yet, Alandra realised, as she wallowed in his look of love for her, she had not told Matt that she loved him. There was so much she wanted to ask, to say, but to tell him that she loved him seemed paramount.

That was why she was the one to feel more shocked than Matt looked, when, on opening her mouth, it was not of her love that she told him but jealousy, which must still have been lingering, had her saying:

'Corinne Hamilton.'

But if Matt was surprised to hear something totally different from what he might have been expecting, he hid it well, as his mouth turned up at the corners, and quietly, he batted back at her:

'Hector Nolan.'

'Hector Nol . . .!' she exclaimed. But she was smiling then. Because from the look of it, if she had been all shades of green about Corinne, then Matt, having asked Hector who was calling that time he had phoned, had been having thoughts that Hector was the unknown man she had said she was in love with.

'Th-there was no other man,' she confessed. 'I lied,' she admitted. And heard, even though Matt looked pleased to hear her say so, that clearly he would not be satisfied until he could file Hector in his 'out' tray.

'So what was Hector Nolan doing ringing you here?'

'It was Hector who brought me here tonight—he's a terrific person,' she said, and seeing Matt didn't look too thrilled at that, she went hurriedly on, 'Happily married, with two lovely children.' She saw he was looking much relieved, and continued. 'I used to work for Hector—he wasn't happy with my replacement. He also happens to be my landlord, so when I posted him my rent and said I was staying with my family, he looked us up in the book and rang to ask me to go back to work for him.'

'Which you did?'

'His new secretary had walked out on him. I fixed up to start work for him that day I went to London.' She paused, then, and just had to ask, her voice hesitant again, 'Why were you so mad that morning, Matt? If—if as you say it wasn't that Grandfather had given me some money?'

'I was as jealous as hell—and not liking it,' he replied. 'You'd told me you were in love with someone, and he had to live in London.' And smiling wryly, 'You didn't help by telling me that some kisses are special.'

'Er—they are,' she said. And at the impish look of her, Matt pulled her to him.

'You wretch,' he breathed, and there was no time for him to say more, for their lips met.

And it was as if he was a man starved of her kisses, as deeply he kissed her, his mouth then travelling her face, his hands tenderly caressing, Alandra holding nothing back as her arms went up and around him. And then his mouth was over hers again.

With each kiss longer than the one before, she was breathless, so that by the time Matt took his mouth from hers she was having enormous trouble to remember what they had been talking about before, or, as for countless moments Matt feasted his eyes on her, if indeed they had been talking about anything.

'Y-you—were jealous?' she managed to recall.

'I've been insane with it,' he confessed, his eyes gentle on her pink cheeks. 'Even before I recognised why it was you were so essential to me—I was jealous. I couldn't even bear that Robbie should teach you to drive.' And while her eyes showed her amazement that *that* was the real reason he had arranged driving lessons for her, he went on to tell her, 'It first started to prick when you had a letter written in a male hand, and then when I picked up the phone and had a man calling himself Hector Nolan asking for you. But it really started to dig into me at that ball we attended in Bedewick. There you were, men lining up to dance with you, and I found myself thinking I'd be damned if I'd join the long queue.'

'But you did dance with me,' she reminded.

'And told myself I was only doing so because I didn't want a type like Frank Millington hanging around Roseacres when he asked you for a date—which I knew he would.' He paused then, and his smile was a shade rueful as he asked, 'Are you going to forgive me my obstinacy? I should have admitted then that I was in love with you—admitted you had started to get under my skin way back when I saw your grandfather had perked up to have you with us and I used him to excuse my asking you to stay.'

'Asking?' she couldn't resist teasing. 'You offered me a thousand pounds!'

'Forgive me,' he said straight away, adding, 'Everything I have is yours.'

Alandra was ready to forgive him anything, but as she smiled, her look revealing as much, Matt's mention of her grandfather had her remembering, and asking:

'What were you doing home from work so early when I phoned? Was it because of Grandfather's birthday?'

'I didn't go to work today,' he said, and explained with a half smile. 'I was on my way out—had just left the breakfast table in fact, when Alain who never plays all his cards in one stroke, casually let drop that he hoped you were going to keep your promise to telephone him today.' Matt couldn't resist a butterfly kiss to her cheek, before he resumed, 'I spent the day in my study with my hand ready to pick up the phone on its first ring.'

'Oh Matt,' she cried, and it was her turn to kiss him shyly as tears stung her eyes at the thought of his waiting all day until she eventually phoned through after four o'clock.

His arms tightened about her and for long moments they kissed and clung. And Alandra thought she would never be as happy again as at this moment. Nor did she feel any less happy when Matt at last pulled back and told her that Hector Nolan was going to have to start looking for another secretary straight away, and memory came to her of Corinne Hamilton.

'Just as Corinne Hamilton is going to have to find another—escort?' she asked. But she was smiling when he answered:

'My darling, I have had very little patience to listen for long to any woman, Corinne Hamilton included, since you left us.'

'You—er—went out a lot,' she said, and wished that she hadn't. But Matt didn't seem to mind that she had been jealous, having had more than his fair share of it, as he replied:

'I couldn't stay in. When you were at home,' oh how that word 'home' thrilled her, 'I knew myself edgy and restless. And when you left us and the house became like a morgue. I just couldn't stay in without you there.' He smiled at her then, and said, 'I did date Corinne once after the ball, trying to make myself believe that all women were the same to me, I think,' he owned. 'But one date with her was sufficient to convince me that she had grown more boring than ever before, and that there was nothing beneath her painted-on beauty than the same avaricious sawdust that ever filled her head.'

Alandra chuckled, her impish grin there as she said, 'You say the sweetest things, Matt.'

His grin matched hers. And then suddenly he was deadly serious as he asked, 'Love me?'

'You know I do,' she replied. And saw him relax, as he said:

'Thank God for that.'

He kissed her then, just once. But oh what a kiss it was! Burning in the fire of passion that came from him, Alandra clutched at him, his body somehow having moved hers until he was over her and pressing her into the settee.

Then abruptly he was pulling her to her feet, his breathing ragged, as he said, 'For Alain's sake we'll have to put in an appearance at dinner. But if we don't go now, my love—if I kiss you again—it will be touch and go if he has his full family at his birthday meal.'

Her cheeks going a warmer crimson than they already were, Alandra knew full well what he meant. But she glanced down at the trousers and shirt she had hurriedly changed into while Hector had been phoning Bianca.

'But I'm not dressed for a birthday dinner!' she said.

But saw as Matt's eyes went over her, fire in them still, that to him she looked perfect. 'Your grandfather will forgive you anything just to see you there,' he said, and his voice had a husky quality to it.

He had to kiss her just once more, and then he had taken hold of her hand and was hurrying her to the door. He did not speak again until he had them both on the landing outside, and the door firmly closed. Then he was putting an arm around her and turning her purposefully towards the stairs, pausing a moment to look down into her shining eyes.

'Particularly,' he said, and seemed as she looked back at him with her heart in her eyes, to have forgotten what he had been about to say. 'Particularly,' he repeated gruffly, 'when he hears what we have to tell him.'

Harlequin® Plus

A WORD ABOUT THE AUTHOR

Jessica Steele was born in Leamington, in England's Midlands, next to the last in a close-knit family of seven children. As a child and young woman, she waged a long battle with illness — but she emerged with a strong spirit that stands her in good stead still.

At a time when things seemed most bleak in her life, Jessica had the good fortune to meet a man who was to become her second husband, Peter. Two years after their marriage, Jessica sat down to try her hand at writing something other than the poetry she had composed for her own satisfaction. Her first attempt at a love story was rejected, and it was then that she began to understand why it was that her mother had often called her a stubborn child. She was to write another seven stories before she was sent the acceptance letter she was waiting for. Her first book was *Spring Girl* (Harlequin Romance #2289), published in 1979.

Throughout it all, her husband was a source of constant encouragement, and when Jessica was able to resign her civil-service job to concentrate on her writing career, it was a credit to the perseverance of them both.